Five variations on a theme . . .

Well, four really. The fifth is just so damn much fun it didn't seem fair to leave it out. We don't know anyone but Keith Laumer who could make Lucifer, a quantum professor, entropy, dimensions, negative-R, luck, devils and a beautiful Samoan girl all hang together so delightfully. And it does have, or could have, something to do with time distortion if you look for it hard enough. But there are still four more for those of you who insist on finding out about honest-to-God time travel. An area in which Keith Laumer is an authority if not a downright originator.

BY KEITH LAUMER

NONFICTION

How to Design and Build Flying Models

GENERAL FICTION

Embassy

SCIENCE FICTION

TIMETRACKS

Keith Laumer

BALLANTINE BOOKS • NEW YORK
An Intext Publisher

SBN 345-02575-X-095

First Printing: April, 1972

Printed in the United States of America

Cover art by Vincent di Fate

BALLANTINE BOOKS, INC.
101 Fifth Avenue, New York, N.Y. 10003

*This book is affectionately dedicated to
Molly and The Little Sister*

THE
TIMESWEEPERS

The man slid into the seat across from me, breathing a little hard, and said, "Do you mind?" He was holding a filled glass in his hand; he waved it at the room, which was crowded, but not that crowded. It was a slightly run-down bar in a run-down street in a run-down world. Just the place for meeting strangers.

I looked him over, not too friendly a look. The smile he was wearing slipped a little and wasn't a smile any more, just a sick smirk. He had a soft, round face, very pale blue eyes, the kind of head that ought to be bald but was covered with a fine blond down like baby chicken feathers. He was wearing a striped sports shirt with a very wide collar laid back over a bulky plaid jacket with padded shoulders and wide lapels. His neck was smooth-skinned, and too thin for his head. The hand that was holding the glass was small and well-lotioned, with short, immaculately manicured fingers. There was a big, cumbersome-looking ring on one of the fingers. The whole composition looked a little out of tune, like something assembled in a hurry by somebody who was short on material and had to make do with what was at hand. Still, it wasn't a

3

bad job, under the circumstances. It had passed—up until now.

"Please don't misunderstand," he said. His voice was like the rest of him: not feminine enough for a woman, but not anything you'd associate with a room full of cigar smoke, either.

"It's vital that I speak with you, Mr. Starv," he went on, talking fast, as if he wanted to get it all said before he was thrown out. "It's a matter of great importance to your future."

He must not have liked what went across my face then; he started to get up and I caught his wrist—as soft and smooth as a baby's—and levered him back into his seat.

"You might as well stay and tell me about it," I said. I looked at him over my glass while he got his smile fixed up and back in position. "My future, eh?" I prompted him. "I wasn't sure I had one."

"Oh, yes," he said, and nodded quickly. "Yes indeed. And I might add that your future is a great deal larger than your past, Mr. Starv."

"Have we met somewhere?"

He shook his head. "Please—I know I don't make a great deal of sense; I'm under a considerable strain. But please listen . . ."

"I'm listening, Mr. . . . what was the name?"

"It really doesn't matter, Mr. Starv. I myself don't enter into the matter at all; I was merely assigned to contact you and deliver the information."

"Assigned?"

He looked at me with an expression like a slave bringing ill tidings to a bad-tempered king.

"Mr. Starv—what would you say if I told you I was a member of a secret organization of supermen?"

"What would you expect me to say?"

"That I'm insane," he said promptly. "Naturally;

that's why I'd prefer to speak directly to the point. Mr. Starv, your life is in danger."

"Go on."

"In precisely—" he glanced at the watch strapped to the underside of his wrist "—one and one half minutes, a man will enter this establishment. He will be dressed in a costume of black, and will carry a cane—ebony, with a silver head. He will go to the bar, order a straight whiskey, drink it, turn, raise the cane and fire three lethal darts into your chest."

I took another swallow of my drink. It was the real stuff; one of the compensations of the job.

"Uh-huh," I said. "Then what?"

"Then? Then?" my little man said rather wildly. "Then you are dead, Mr. Starv!" He leaned across the table and threw this at me in a hiss, with quite a lot of spit.

"Well, I guess that's that," I said.

"No!" His fat little hand shot out and clutched my arm with more power than I'd given him credit for. "This is what will happen—*unless* you act at once to avert it."

"I take it that's where the big future you mentioned comes in."

"Mr. Starv, you must leave here at once." He fumbled in a pocket of his coat, brought out a card with an address printed on it: *309 Turkon Place.*

"It's an old building, very stable, quite near here. Go to the third floor. You'll have to climb a wooden stairway, but it's quite safe. A door marked with the numeral 9 is at the back. Enter the room and wait."

"Why would I do that?" I asked him.

He wiped at his face with his free hand.

"In order to save your life," he said.

"What's the idea—that the boy in black can't work in rooms marked 9?"

"Please, Mr. Starv—time is short. Won't you simply trust me?"

"Where'd you get my name?"

"Does that matter more than your life?"

"The name's a phony. I made it up about an hour and a half ago, when I registered at the hotel across the street."

His earnest look went all to pieces; he was still trying to reassemble it when the street door of the bar opened and a man in a black overcoat, black velvet collar, black homburg and carrying a black swagger stick walked in.

My new chum's fingers clamped into the same grooves they'd made last time.

"You see? Just as I said. Now, quickly, Mr. Starv—"

I brushed his hand off me and slid out of the booth. The man in black went to the bar without looking my way, took a stool near the end.

I went across and took the stool on his left.

He didn't look at me. He was so busy not looking at me that he didn't even look around when my elbow dug into his side. If there was a gun in his pocket, I couldn't feel it.

I leaned a little toward him. "Who is he?" I said, about eight inches from his ear. His head jerked. He put his hands on the bar and turned. His face was thin, white around the nostrils from anger or illness, gray everywhere else. His eyes looked like little black stones.

"Are you addressing me?" he said in a tone with a chill like Scott's last camp on the ice cap.

"Your friend with the sticky hands is waiting over in the booth. Why not join the party?"

"You've made an error," Blackie said, and turned away.

From the corner of my eye I saw the other half of the team trying a sneak play around left end. I caught him a few yards past the door.

It was a cold night. Half an inch of snow squeaked under our shoes as he tried to jerk free of the grip I took on his upper arm.

"Tell me about it," I said. "After I bought the mind-reading act, what was to come next?"

"You fool—I'm trying to save your life—have you no sense of gratitude?"

"What made it worth the trouble? My suit wouldn't fit you, and the cash in my pocket wouldn't pay cab fare over to Turkon Place and back."

"Let me go! We must get off the street!" He tried to kick my ankle, and I socked him under the ribs hard enough to fold him against me, wheezing like a bagpipe. I took a quick step back and heard the flat *whak!* of a silenced pistol and the whisper that a bullet makes when it passes an inch from your ear: Blackie's cane going into action from the door to the bar.

There was an alley mouth a few feet away. We made it in one jump. My little pal had his feet working again, and tried to use them to wreck my knee. I had to bruise his shins a little.

"Easy," I told him. "That slug changes things. Quiet down and I'll let go of your neck."

He nodded as well as he could with my thumb where it was and I eased him back against the wall. I put my back against it, beside him, with him between me and the alley mouth. I made a little production of levering back the hammer of my Mauser.

Two or three minutes went past like geologic ages.

"We'll take a look. You first." I prodded him forward. Nobody shot at him. I risked a look. Except for a few people not in black overcoats, the sidewalk was empty.

My car was across the street. I walked him across and waited while he got in and slid across under the wheel, then got in after him. There were other parked cars, and plenty of dark windows up above for a sniper to work from, but nobody did.

"309 Turkon Place, you said." I nudged him with the Mauser. "Let's go have a look."

He drove badly, like a middle-aged widow who only learned to drive after her husband died. We clashed gears and ran stoplights across town to the street he had named. It was a badly-lit unpatched brick dead end that rose steeply toward a tangle of telephone poles at the top. The house was tall and narrow, slanted against the sky, showing no lights. I prodded my guide ahead of me along the narrow walk that ran back beside the house, went in via the back door. It resisted a little, but gave without making any more noise than a dropped xylophone.

We stood on some warped linoleum and smelled last week's cabbage and listened to some dense silence.

"Don't be afraid," the little man said. "There's no one here." He led me along a passage a little wider than my elbows, past a tarnished mirror and a stand full of umbrellas, up steep steps with black rubber matting held by tarnished brass rods. The flooring creaked on the landing. Another flight brought us into a low-ceilinged hall with gray-painted doors made visible by the pale light coming through a wire-glass skylight.

He found number 9, put an ear against it, opened up and went in. I followed.

It was a small bedroom with a double bed, a dresser with a doily on it, a straight chair, a rocker, an oval rag rug, a hanging fixture in the center with a colored glass bowl. My host placed the chairs into a cozy *tête-a-tête* arrangement, offered me the rocker, and perched on the edge of the other.

"Now," he said, and put his fingertips together comfortably, like a pawnbroker about to beat you down on the value of the family jewels, "I suppose you want to hear all about the man in black, how I knew just when he'd appear, and so on."

"It was neat routine," I said. "Up to a point. After you fingered me, if I didn't buy the act, Blackie would plug me—with a dope dart. If I did—I'd be so grateful I'd come here."

"As indeed you have." My little man looked different now, more relaxed, less eager to please. "I suppose I need not add that the end result will be the same." He made a nice hip draw and showed me a strange looking little gun, all shiny rods and levers.

"You will now tell me about yourself, Mr. Starv—or whatever you may choose to call yourself."

"Wrong again—Karge," I said.

For an instant it didn't register. Then his fingers twitched and the gun made a spitting sound and needles showered off my chest. I let him fire the full magazine. Then I shot him under the left eye with the pistol I had palmed while he was settling himself on his chair.

He settled further; his head was bent over his left shoulder as if he were trying to admire the water spots on the ceiling. His little pudgy hands opened and closed a couple of times. He leaned sideways quite slowly and hit the floor like a hundred and fifty pounds of heavy machinery.

Which he was, of course.

The shots hadn't made much noise—no more than the one fired at me by the Enforcer had. I listened, heard nothing in the way of a response. I laid the Karge out on his back—or on *its* back—and cut the seal on his reel compartment, lifted out the tape he'd been operating on. It was almost spent, indicating that his mission had been almost completed. I checked his pockets but turned up nothing, not even a ball of lint.

It took me twenty minutes to go over the room. I found a brain-reader focused on the rocker from the stained-glass ceiling light. He'd gone to a lot of effort to make sure he cleaned me before disposing of the remains.

I took time to record my scan to four point detail, then went back down to the street. A big, square car went past, making a lot of noise in the silent street, but no bullets squirted from it. I checked my locator and started east, downslope.

It was a twenty-minute walk to the nearest spot the gauges said was within the acceptable point-point range for a locus transfer. I tapped out the code with my tongue against the trick molars set in my lower jaw, felt the silent impact of temporal implosion, and was squinting against the dazzling sunlight glaring down on Dinosaur Beach.

My game of cat-and-mouse with the Karge had covered several square miles of the city of Buffalo, New York, T.F. late March, 1936. A quick review of my movements from the time of my arrival at the locus told me that the Timecast station should be about a mile and a half distant to the southwest, along the beach. I discarded the warmer portions of my costume and started hiking.

The sea in this era—some sixty-five million years B.C.—was south-sea-island blue, stretching wide and placid to the horizon. The long swells coming in off the Eastern Ocean—which would one day become the Atlantic—crashed on the gray sand with the same familiar *crump-booom!* that I had known in a dozen Eras. It was a comforting sound. It said that after all, the doings of the little creatures that scuttled on her shores were nothing much in the life of Mother Ocean, age five billion and not yet in her prime.

There was a low headland just ahead, from which the station would be visible a mile or so beyond: a small, low, gray-white structure perched on the sand above high tide line, surrounded by tree ferns and club mosses, not as decoration but to render the installation as inconspicuous as possible, on the theory that if the wild life were either attracted or repelled by the strangeness it might introduce an uncharted U-line on the probability charts which would render a thousand years of painstaking— and painful—temporal mapping invalid.

Inside, Nel Jard, the Chief Timecaster, would have me in for debriefing, would punch his notes into the master plot, and wave me on my way back to Nexx Central where a new job would be waiting, having nothing to do with the last one. I'd never learn just why the Karge had been placed where it was, what sort of deal it had made with the Enforcers, what part the whole thing played in the larger tapestry of the Nexx grand strategy.

That's what would have happened. Except that I topped the rise just then and saw the long curve of beach ahead, and the tongue of jungle that stretched down almost to the shore along the ridge. But where the station had been, there was nothing but a smoking crater.

Dinosaur Beach had been so named because a troop of small allosaur-like reptiles had been scurrying along it when the first siting party had fixed-in there. That had been sixty years ago, Nexx Subjective, only a few months after the decision to implement Project Timesweep.

The idea wasn't without merit. The First Era of time travel had closely resembled the dawn of the space age in some ways—notably, in the trail of rubbish it left behind. In the case of the space garbage, it had taken half a dozen major collisions to convince the authorities of the need to sweep circumterrestrial space clean of fifty years' debris in the form of spent rocket casings, defunct telemetry gear, and derelict relay satellites long lost track of. In the process they'd turned up a large number of odds and ends of meteoric rock and iron, a few lumps of clearly terrestrial origin, possibly volcanic, the mummified body of an astronaut lost on an early space walk, and a couple of artifacts that the authorities of the day had scratched their heads over and finally written off as the equivalent of empty beer cans tossed out by visitors from out-system.

That was before the days of Timecasting, of course.

The Timesweep program was a close parallel to the space sweep. The Old Era temporal experimenters had littered the time-ways with everything from early one-way timecans to observation stations, dead bodies, abandoned instruments, weapons and equipment of all sorts, including an automatic mining setup established under the Antarctic ice which caused headaches at the time of the Big Melt.

Then the three hundred years of the Last Peace put an end to that; and when temporal transfer was rediscovered in early New Era times, the lesson had been heeded. Rigid rules were enforced from the beginning of the Second Program, forbidding all the mistakes that had been made by the First Program pioneers.

Which meant the Second Program had to invent its own disasters—like the one I was looking at.

I had gone flat on the hot sand at first sight of the pit among the blackened stumps of the club mosses, while a flood of extraneous thoughts went whirling through my tired old brain, as thoughts will in such moments. I had been primed to step out of the heat and the insects and the sand into cool, clean air, soft music, the luxury of a stimbath and a nap on a real air couch.

But that was all gone to slag now. I hugged the ground and looked down at it and tried to extract what data I could from what I could see. It wasn't much.

Item one: Some power had had the will and the way to blast a second-class Nexx staging station out of existence. It seemed they'd used good old-fashioned nuclears for the job, too; nothing so subtle as a temporal lift, or a phase-suppressor.

Item two: The chore had been handled during the ten days N.S. I'd been on location in 1936. There might or might not be some message there for me.

I suppressed the desire to jump up and run down for a closer look. I stayed where I was, playing boulder, and looked at the scene some more with gritty eyes that wept copiously in the glare of the tropical Jurassic sun. I didn't see anything move —which didn't mean there was nothing there to see. After half an hour of that, I got up and walked down to the ruins.

"Ruins" was an exaggeration. There was a fused glass pit a hundred yards in diameter surrounded by charred organic matter. That gave me item three:

Nothing had survived—no people, no equipment. Not only would I not have the benefit of soft music and bed to match, there'd be no debriefing, no input of data into the master tape, no replay of the Karge operation tape to give me a clue to Enforcer Strategy. And worst of all, there'd be no outjump to Nexx Central.

Which made things a trifle awkward, since the location of Central was a secret buried under twelve layers of interlocked ciphers in the main tank of the Nexial Brain. Not even the men who built the installation knew its physical and temporal coordinates. The only way to reach it was to be computer-routed via one of the hundred and twelve official staging stations scattered across Old Era time. And not just any station: it had to be the one my personal jumper field was attuned to.

Which was a thin layer of green glass lining a hollow in the sand.

It was one of those times when the mind goes racing around inside the trap of the skull like a mouse in a bucket, making frantic leaps for freedom and falling back painfully on its rear.

On about the tenth lap, an idea bobbed up and grinned a rather ghastly grin.

My personal jump gear, being installed in my body, was intact. All I lacked was a target. But that didn't mean I couldn't jump. All it meant was that I wouldn't know where I'd land—if anywhere.

There had been a lot of horror stories circulated back at Nexx Central about what had happened to people who misfired on a jump. They ranged from piecemeal reception at a dozen stations strung out across a few centuries, to disembodied voices screaming to be let out. Also, there were several rules against it.

The alternative was to set up housekeeping here on the beach, with or without dinosaurs, and hope that a rescue mission arrived before I died of old age, heat, thirst, or reptiles.

I didn't like the odds, but they were all the odds I had.

I took a final breath of humid beach air, a last look around at the bright, brutal view of sea and sand, the high, empty sky. It seemed to be waiting for something to happen.

The tune I played on the console set in my jaw was different this time, but the effect was much the same: The painless blow of a silent club, the sense of looping the loop through a Universe-sized Klein bottle—

Total darkness and a roar of sound like Niagara Falls going over me in a barrel.

For a few seconds I stood absolutely still, taking a swift inventory of my existence. I seemed to be all here, organized pretty much as usual. The sound went on, the blackness failed to fade. The rule book said that in a case of transfer malfunction to remain immobile and await retrieval, but in this case that might take quite a while. Also, there was the datum that no one had ever lived to report a jump malfunction, which suggested that possibly the rule book was wrong.

I tried to breathe, and nothing happened. That decided me. I took a step and emerged as through a curtain into a strange blackish light, shot through with little points of dazzling brilliance, like what you see just before you faint from loss of blood. But before I could put my head between my knees, the dazzle faded and I was looking at the jump room of a regulation Nexx Staging Station. And I could breathe.

I did that for a few moments, then turned and looked at the curtain I had come through. It was a solid wall of beryl-steel, to my knowledge over two meters thick.

Maybe the sound I had heard was the whizzing of molecules of dense metal interpenetrating with my own two hundred pounds of impure water. That was a phenomenon I'd have to let ride until later. More pressing business called for attention first— such as discovering why the station was as silent as King Sethy's tomb after the grave robbers finished with it.

It took me ten minutes to check every room on operations level. Nobody was home. The same for the R and R complex. Likewise the equipment division, and the power chamber.

The core sink was drawing normal power, the charge was up on the transmitter plates, the green lights were on all across the panels; but nothing was tapping the station for so much as a microerg.

Which was impossible. The links that tied a staging station to Nexx Central and in turn monitored the activities of personnel operating out of the station always drew at least a trickle of carrier power. They had to, as long as the station existed. A no-drain condition was impossible anywhere in normal space time.

I didn't like the conclusion, but I reached it anyway.

All the stations were identical; in fact, considering their mass-production by the time-stutter process which distributed them up and down the temporal contour, there's a school of thought that holds that they *are* identical; alternate temporal aspects of the same physical matrix. But that was theory, and my present situation was fact. A fact I had to deal with.

I went along the passage to the entry lock—some of the sites are hostile to what Nexx thinks of as ordinary life—circled it, and almost stepped out.

Not quite.

The ground ended about ten feet from the out-flung entry wing. Beyond was a pearly gray mist, swirling against an invisible barrier. I went forward to the edge and lay flat and looked over. I could see the curve of the underside of the patch of solid rock the station perched on. It was as smooth and polished as green glass. Like the green glass crater I'd seen back on the beach.

The station had been scooped out of the rock like a giant dip of ice cream and deposited here, behind a barrier of a kind the scientists of Nexx Central had never dreamed of.

That gave me two or three things to think of. I thought of them while I went back in through the lock, and down the transit tunnel to the transfer booth.

It looked normal. Aside from the absence of a cheery green light to tell me that the field was on sharp focus to Nexx Central, all was as it should be. The plates were hot, the dial readings normal.

If I stepped inside, I'd be transferred—somewhere.

Some more interesting questions suggested themselves, but I'd already been all over those. I stepped in and the door valved shut and I was alone with my thoughts. Before I could have too many of those I reached out and tripped the Xmit button.

A soundless bomb blew me motionlessly across dimensionless space.

A sense of vertigo that slowly faded; a shimmer of light, as from a reflective surface in constant, restless movement; a hollow, almost metallic sound, coming from below me; a faint sensation of heat and pressure against my side . . .

Sunlight shining on water. The waves slapping the hollow steel pilings of a pier. The pressure of a plank deck on which I was lying—a remote, tentative pressure, like a sun-warmed cloud.

I sat up. The horizon pivoted to lie flat, dancing in the heat-ripples. The spars and masts of a small sailing ship poked up bare against a lush blue sky.

Not a galleon, I realized—at least not a real one. The steel pilings rendered that anachronous. That made it a replica, probably from the Revival, circa 2020 A.D. I got to my feet, noticing a curious tendency on the part of my feet to sink into the decking.

I was still dizzy from the shock of the transfer. Otherwise I would probably have stayed where I was until I had sorted through the ramifications of this latest development. Instead, I started toward the end of the pier. It was high and wide—about twenty feet from edge to edge, fifteen feet above the water. From the end I could look down on the deck of the pseudo-galleon, snuggled up close against the resilient bumper at the end of the quay. It was a fine reproduction, artfully carved and weather-scarred. Probably with a small reactor below decks, steel armor under the near-oak hull planking, and luxury accommodations for an operator and a dozen holiday-makers.

Then I saw the dead man lying on the deck. He was face-down at the foot of the mast—a big fellow dressed in sixteenth century costume, soiled and sweat-stained. He looked much too authentic to be part of a game.

I stood still and tried to get it together. Something about what I was looking at bothered me. I wanted to see it more closely. A ladder went down. I descended, jumped the six-foot gap. Nobody came out to see what the disturbance was all about.

The mast cast a black shadow across the hand-hewn deck, across the man lying there, one hand under him, the other outflung. A gun lay a yard from the empty hand. There was a lot of soggy black lace in a black puddle under his throat.

I picked up the gun. It was much heavier than a gun had any right to be. It was a .01 micro jetgun of Nexx manufacture, with a grip that fitted my hand perfectly.

It ought to. It was my gun. I looked at the hand it had fallen from. It looked like my hand. I didn't like doing it, but I turned the body over and looked at the face.

It was my face.

The post-mission conditioning that had wiped the whole sequence from my memory—standard practice after a field assignment—broke.

I remembered it now, the whole sequence: the capture of the Karge-operated ship which had been operating in New Spanish waters, the flight across the decks in company with a party of English seamen, the cornering of the android—

But it hadn't ended like this. I had shot the Karge, not the reverse. I had brought the captive vessel—a specially-equipped Karge operations unit in disguise—to the bulk transfer point at Locus Q-997, from which it had been transmitted back to Nexx Central for total intelligence analysis.

But here it was, still tied to the pier at the transfer station. With me lying on the deck, very dead indeed from a large-caliber bullet through the throat.

Something was very wrong. It hadn't happened that way—not in my time track. Then, suddenly, I understood the magnitude of the trap I had blundered into.

A Nexx agent is a hard man to get rid of: hard to kill, hard to immobilize, because he's protected by all the devices of a rather advanced science.

But if he can be marooned in the closed loop of an unrealized alternate reality—a pseudo-reality from which there can be no outlet to a future which doesn't exist—then he's out of action forever.

I could live a long time here. There'd be food and water and a place to sleep; but no escape, ever; no trace on any recording instrument to show where I had gone. . . .

But I wouldn't dwell on that particular line of thought right now—not yet. Not until it was the only thought left for me to have. Like a locked-out motorist patting his pockets three times looking for the key he can see hanging in the ignition, I patted my mental pockets looking for an out.

I didn't like the one I found, but I liked it better than not finding it.

My personal jump mechanism was built into me, tuned to me. And its duplicate was built into the corpse lying at my feet. Just what it might be focused on was an open question; it would depend on what had been in the dead man's mind at the instant of death.

The circuitry of the jump device—from antennae to power coils—consisted largely of the nervous system of the owner. Whether it was still functional depended on how long "I" had been dead. I squatted and put two fingers against the dead neck.

Barely cool. It only takes five minutes without oxygen for irreversible brain damage to occur.

What effect that would have was a mystery, but there was no time to weigh odds.

The corpse's jaws were locked hard, fortunately in a half-open position. I got a finger inside and tried my code on the molar installation.

A giant clapped his hands together, with me in the middle.

Twilight, on a curved, tree-shaded street. Autumn leaves underfoot, clotted against the curbing, and blowing in the cold, wet wind. Low buildings set well back, with soft light coming from the windows. Tended lawns and gardens, polished automobiles in hedge-lined drives. I was directly opposite the front door of a gray field stone house. The door opened. *I* stepped out.

This time I was prepared. Not really prepared, but half expecting it, like an unlucky card player turning up a losing card.

Time: About ten years earlier, N.S. Or the year 1968, local. Place, a village in the mid-western U.S.A. I had jumped back into my own past—one of my first assignments, long ago completed, filed in the master tape, a part of Timesweep history.

But not any more. The case was reopened on the submission of new evidence. I was doubled back on my own time track.

The fact that this was a violation of every natural law governing time travel was only a minor aspect of the situation.

The past that Nexx Central had painfully rebuilt to eliminate the disastrous results of Old Era time meddling was coming unstuck.

And if one piece of the new mosaic that was being so carefully assembled was coming unglued—then everything that had been built on it was likewise on the skids, ready to slide down and let the whole complex and artificial structure collapse in a heap of temporal rubble that neither Nexx Central or anyone else would be able to salvage.

With the proper lever, you can move worlds; but you need a solid place to stand. That had been Nexx Central's job for the past six decades: to build a platform in the remote pre-Era on which all the later structure would be built.

And it looked as though it had failed.

I watched myself—ten years younger—step out into the chilly twilight, close the door, through which I caught just a glimpse of a cozy room, and a pretty girl smiling goodbye. My alter ego turned toward the upper end of the street, set off at a brisk walk. I placed the time then.

I had spent three months in the village, from late summer to autumn. The job had been a waiting game, giving the local Karge time to betray himself. He had done so, and I had spotted it; a too-clever craftsman, turning out hand tools, the design of which was based on alloys and principles that wouldn't be invented for another century.

I had done my job and made my report and been ordered back. I had wanted to explain to Lisa, the girl in the house; but, of course, that had been impossible. I had stepped out for a six-pack of ale, and had never come back. It was common sense, as well as regulations, but my heart wasn't in it. Her face had haunted me as I left to go to the point-point site for transfer back to Central.

As it was haunting the other me now. This was that last night. I was on my way back to Nexx Central now. It would be a ten-minute walk into the forest that grew down to the outskirts of the village. There I would activate the jump field and leave the twentieth century ten thousand years behind. And an hour later even the memory would be gone.

I picked the darkest side of the street and followed myself toward the woods.

I caught up with myself mooching around in the tangle of wild berry bushes I remembered from last time, homing in on the optimum signal from my locator. This had been my first field transfer, and I hadn't been totally certain the system would work.

I came up fast, skirted the position and worked my way up to within twenty feet of take-off position. The other me was looking nervous and unhappy, a feeling I fully sympathized with.

I gained another six feet, smooth and quiet. I'd learned a lot of field technique since the last time I'd been on this spot. I watched the other me brace himself, grit my teeth, and tap out the code—

Two jumps, and I was behind *me;* I grabbed *me* by both leather sleeves from behind, up high, slammed *my* elbows together, whirled *me,* and gave *me* a hearty shove into the brambles just as the field closed around me, and threw me a million miles down a dark tunnel full of solid rock.

Someone was shaking me. I tried to summon up enough strength for a groan, didn't make it, opened my eyes instead.

I was looking up into my own face.

For a few whirly instants I thought the younger me had made a nice comeback from the berry bushes and laid me out from behind.

Then I noticed the lines in the face, and the hollow cheeks. The clothes this new me was wearing were identical with the ones I had on, except for being somewhat more travel stained. And there was a nice bruise above the right eye that I didn't remember getting.

"Listen carefully," my voice said to me. "I've come full circle. Dead end. Closed loop. No way out—except one—maybe. I don't like it much, but I don't see any alternative. Last time around, we had the same talk—but I was on the floor then, and another version of us was here ahead of me with the same proposal. I didn't like it. I thought there had to be another way. I went on—and wound up back here. Only this time *I'm* the welcoming committee."

He unholstered the gun at his hip and held it out.

"I . . . *we're* . . . being . . . manipulated. All the evidence shows that. I don't know what the objective is but we have to break the cycle. *You* have to break it. Take this and shoot me through the head."

I got up on my elbows, which was easier than packing a grand piano up the Matterhorn, and shook my head, both in negation and to clear some of the fog. That was a mistake. It just made it throb worse.

"I know all the arguments," my future self was saying. "I used them myself, about ten days ago. That's the size of this little temporal enclave we have all to ourselves. But they're no good. This is the one real change we can introduce."

"You're out of your mind," I said. "I'm not the suicidal type—even if the me I'm killing is you."

"That's what they're counting on. It worked, too, with me. I wouldn't do it." He . . . *I* . . . weighed the gun on his palm and looked at me very coldly indeed.

"If I thought shooting you would help, I'd do it without a tremor," he said. He was definitely *he* now.

"Why don't you?"

"Because the next room is full of bones," he said

with a smile that wasn't pretty. "Our bones. Plus the latest addition, which still has a little spoiled meat on it. That's what's in store for me. Starvation. So it's up to you."

"Nightmare," I said, and started to lie back and try for a pleasanter dream.

"Uh-huh—but you're awake," he said, and caught my hand and shoved the gun into it.

"Do it now—before I lose my nerve!"

I made quite a bit of noise groaning, getting to my feet. I ached all over.

"You weren't quite in focal position on the jump here," he explained to me. "You cracked like a whip. Lucky nothing's seriously dislocated."

"Let's talk a little sense," I said. "Killing you won't change anything. What I could do alone we could do better together."

"Wrong. This is a jump station, or a mirror-image of one. Complete except for the small detail that the jump field's operating in a closed loop. Outside, there's nothing."

"You mean—this is the same—"

"Right. That was the first time around. You jumped out into a non-object dead end. You were smart, you figured a way out—but they were ahead of us there, too. The circle's still closed—and here you are. You can jump out again, and repeat the process. That's all."

"Suppose I jump back to the wharf and *don't* use the corpse's jump gear—"

"Then you'll starve there."

"All right; suppose I make the second jump, but don't clobber myself—"

"Same result. He leaves, you're stranded."

"Maybe not. There'd be food there. I could survive, maybe eventually be picked up—"

"Negative. I've been all over that. You'd die

there. Maybe after a long life, or maybe a short one. Same result."

"What good will shooting you do?"

"I'm not sure. But it would introduce a brand new element into the equation—like cheating at solitaire."

I argued a little more. He took me on a tour of the station. I looked out at the pearly mist, poked into various rooms. Then he showed me the bone room.

I think the smell convinced me.

I lifted the gun and flipped off the safety.

"Turn around," I snapped at him. He did.

"There's one consoling possibility," he said. "This might have the effect of—"

The shot cut off whatever it was he was going to say, knocked him forward as if he'd been jerked by a rope around the neck. I got just a quick flash of the hole I'd blown in the back of his skull before a fire that blazed brighter than the sun leaped up in my brain and burned away the walls that had caged me in.

I was a giant eye, looking down on a tiny stage. I saw myself, an agent of Nexx Central, moving through the scenes of ancient Buffalo, weaving my petty net around the Karge. *Karge,* a corruption of "cargo," referring to the legal decision as to the status of the machine-men in the great Transport Accommodations riots of the mid Twenty-eighth Century.

Karges, lifeless machines, sent back from the Third Era in the second great Timesweep, attempting to correct not only the carnage irresponsibly strewn by the primitive Old Era temporal explorers, but to eliminate the even more destructive effects of the New Era Timesweep Enforcers.

The Third Era had recognized the impossibility of correcting the effects of human interference with more human interference.

Machines which registered neutral on the life-balance scales could do what men could not—could restore the integrity of the Temporal Core.

Or so they thought.

After the Great Collapse and the long night that followed, Nexx Central had arisen to control the Fourth Era. They saw that the tamperings of prior eras were all a part of the grand pattern; that any effort to manipulate reality via temporal policing was doomed only to weaken the temporal fabric.

Thus, my job as a field agent of Nexx: To cancel out the efforts of all of them; to allow the wound in time to heal; for the great stem of Life to grow strong again.

How foolish it all seemed now. Was it possible that the theoreticians of Nexx Central failed to recognize that their own efforts were no different from those of earlier Timesweepers? And that . . .

There was another thought there, a vast one; but before I could grasp it, the instant of insight faded and left me standing over the body of the murdered man, with a wisp of smoke curling from the gun in my hand and the echoes of something immeasurable and beyond value ringing down the corridors of my brain. And out of the echoes, one clear realization emerged: Timesweeping was a fallacy; but it was a fallacy practiced not only by the experimenters of the New Era and the misguided fixers of the Third Era, but also by the experts of Nexx Central.

There was, also, another power.

A power greater than Nexx Central, that had tried to sweep me under the rug—and had almost made it. I had been manipulated as neatly as I had maneuvered the Karge and the Enforcer, back in Buffalo. I had been hurried along, kept off balance, shunted into a closed cycle which should have taken me out of play for all time.

As it would have, if there hadn't been one small factor that they had missed.

My alter ego had died in my presence—and his mind-field, in the instant of the destruction of the organic generator which created and supported it, had jumped too, merged with mine.

For a fraction of a second, I had enjoyed an operative IQ which I estimated at a minimum of 250.

And while I was still mulling over the ramifications of that realization, the walls faded around me and I was standing in the receptor vault at Nexx Central.

There was the cold glare of the high ceiling on white walls, the hum of the field-focusing coils, the sharp odors of ozone and hot metal in the air—all familiar, if not homey. What wasn't familiar was the squad of armed men in the gray uniforms of Nexx security guards. They were formed up in a circle, with me at the center; and in every pair of hands was an implosion rifle, aimed at my head. An orange light shone in my face—a damper field projector.

I got the idea. I raised my hands—slowly. One man came in and frisked me, lifted my gun and several other items of external equipment. The captain motioned. Keeping formation, they walked me out of the vault, along a corridor, through two sets of armored doors and onto a stretch of gray carpet before the wide, flat desk of the Timecaster in Charge, Nexx Central.

He was a broad, square-faced, powerful man, clear-featured, his intellect as incisive as his speech. He dismissed the guard—all but two—and pointed to a chair.

"Sit down, Agent," he said. I sat.

"You deviated from your instructions," he said. There was no anger in his tone, no accusation, not even any curiosity.

"That's right, I did," I said.

"Your mission was the execution of the Enforcer DVK-Z-97, with the ancillary goal of capture, intact, of a Karge operative unit, Series H, ID 453." He said it as though I hadn't spoken. This time I didn't answer.

"You failed to effect the capture," he went on. "Instead, you destroyed the Karge brain. And you made no effort to carry out the execution of the Enforcer."

What he said was true. There was no point in denying it, any more than there was in confirming it.

"Since no basis for such actions within the framework of your known psychindex exists, it is clear that your motives must be sought outside the context of the Nexx policy. Clearly, any assumption involving your subversion by prior temporal powers is insupportable. Ergo—you represent a force not yet in subjective existence."

"Isn't that a case of trying to wag the dog with the tail?" I said. "You're postulating a Fifth Era just to give me a motive. Maybe I just fouled up the assignment. Maybe I went off my skids. Maybe—"

"You may drop the Old Era persona now, Agent. Aside from the deductive conclusion, I have the evidence of your accidentally revealed intellectual resources. In the moment of crisis, you registered in the third psychometric range. No human brain known to have existed has ever attained that level. I point this out so as to make plain to you the fruitlessness of denying the obvious."

"I was wrong," I said. "You're not postulating a Fifth Era."

He looked mildly interested.

"You're postulating a Sixth Era," I went on.

"What is the basis for that astonishing statement?" he said, not looking astonished.

"Easy," I said. "*You*'re Fifth Era. I should have seen it sooner. You've infiltrated Nexx Central."

"And you've infiltrated our infiltration. That is unfortunate. Our operation has been remarkably successful so far, but no irreparable harm has been done—although you realized your situation, of course, as soon as you found yourself isolated—I use the term imprecisely—in the aborted station."

"I started to get the idea then," I told him. "I was sure when I saw the direction the loop was taking me. Nexx Central had to be involved. But it was a direct sabotage of Nexx policy; so infiltration was the obvious answer."

"Fortunate that your thinking didn't lead you one step further," he said. "If you had eluded my recovery probe, the work of millennia might have been destroyed."

"Futile work," I said.

"Indeed? Perhaps you're wrong, Agent. Accepting the apparent conclusion that you represent a Sixth Era does not necessarily imply your superiority. Retrogressions *have* occurred in history."

"Not this time."

"Nonetheless—here you are."

"Use your head," I said. "Your operation's been based on the proposition that your Era, being later, can see pitfalls the Nexx people couldn't. Doesn't it follow that a later Era can see *your* mistakes?"

"We are making no mistakes."

"If you weren't, I wouldn't be here."

"Impossible!" he said as if he meant it. "For four thousand years a process of disintegration has proceeded, abetted by every effort to undo it. When man first interfered with the orderly flow of time, he sowed the seeds of eventual dissolution. By breaking open the entropic channel he allowed the incalculable forces of temporal progression to diffuse across an infinite spectrum of progressively weaker matrices. Life is a product of time. When the density of the temporal flux falls below a critical value, life ends. Our intention is to prevent that ultimate tragedy."

"You can't rebuild a past that never was," I said.

"That is not our objective. Ours is a broad program of reknitting the temporal fabric by bringing together previously divergent trends. We are apolitical; we support no ideology. We are content to preserve the vitality of the continuum. As for yourself, I have one question to ask you, Agent." He frowned at me. "Not an agent of Nexx, but nonetheless an agent. Tell me: What motivation could your Era have for working to destroy the reality core on which any conceivable future *must* depend?"

"The first Timesweepers set out to undo the mistakes of the past," I said. "Those who came after them found themselves faced with a bigger job: cleaning up after the cleaners-up. Nexx Central tried to take the broad view, to put it all back where it was before any of the meddling started. Now you're even more ambitious. You're using Nexx Central to manipulate not the past, but the future—in other words, the Sixth Era. You should have expected that program wouldn't be allowed to go far."

"Are you attempting to tell me that any effort to undo the damage, to reverse the trend toward dissolution, is doomed?"

"As long as man tries to put a harness on his own destiny, he'll defeat himself. Every petty dictator who ever tried to enforce a total state discovered that, in his own small way. The secret of man is his unchainabilty; his existence depends on uncertainty, insecurity—the chance factor. Take that away and you take all."

"This is a doctrine of failure and defeat," he said flatly. "A dangerous doctrine. It will now be necessary for you to inform me fully as to your principals: who sent you here, who directs your actions, where your base of operations is located. Everything."

"I don't think so."

"You feel very secure, Agent. You, you tell yourself, represent a more advanced Era, and are thus the immeasurable superior of any more primitive power. But a muscular fool may chain a genius. I have trapped you here. We are now safely enclosed in an achronic enclave of zero temporal dimensions, totally divorced from any conceivable outside influence. You will find that you are effectively immobilized; any suicide equipments you may possess are useless, as is any temporal transfer device. And even were you to die, your brain will be instantly tapped and drained of all knowledge, both at conscious and subconscious levels."

"You're quite thorough," I said, "but not quite thorough enough. You covered yourself from the outside—but not from the inside."

He frowned; he didn't like that remark. He sat up straighter in his chair and made a curt gesture to his gun-handlers on either side of me. I knew his next words would be the kill order. Before he could say them, I triggered the thought-code that had been waiting under several levels of deep hypnosis for this moment. He froze just like that, with his mouth open and a look of deep bewilderment in his eyes.

The eclipse-like light of null-time stasis shone on his taut face, on the faces of the two armed men standing rigid with their fingers already tightening on their firing studs. I went between them, fighting the walking-through-syrup sensation, and out into the passage. The only sound was the slow, all-pervasive, metronome-like beat that some theoreticians said represented the basic frequency rate of the creation/destruction cycle of reality.

I checked the transfer room first, then every other compartment of the station. The Fifth Era infiltrators had done their work well. There was nothing here to give any indication of how far in the subjective future their operation was based, no clues to the extent of their penetration of Nexx Central's sweep programs. This was data that would have been of interest, but wasn't essential. I had accomplished phase one of my basic mission: smoking out the random factor that had been creating anomalies in the long-range time maps for the era.

Of a total of one hundred and twelve personnel in the station, four were Fifth Era transferees, a fact made obvious in the stasis condition by the distinctive aura that their abnormally high temporal potential created around them. I carried out a mind-wipe on pertinent memory sectors and triggered them back to their loci of origin. There would be a certain amount of head-scratching and equipment re-examining when the original effort to jump them back to their assignments at Nexx Central apparently failed; but as far as temporal operations were concerned, all four were permanently out of action, trapped in the same type of closed-loop phenomenon they had tried to use on me.

The files called for my attention next. I carried out a tape scan *in situ*, edited the records to eliminate all evidence that might lead Third Era personnel into undesirable areas of speculation.

I was just finishing up the chore when I heard the sound of footsteps in the corridor outside the record center.

Aside from the fact that nothing not encased in an eddy field like the one that allowed me to operate in null-time could move here, the intrusion wasn't too surprising. I had been expecting a visitor of some sort. The situation almost demanded it.

He came through the door, a tall, fine-featured, totally hairless man elegantly dressed in a scarlet suit with deep purple brocaded designs worked all over it, like eels coiling through seaweed. He gave the room one of those flick-flick glances that prints the whole picture on the brian to ten decimals in a one microsecond gestalt, nodded to me as if I were a casual acquaintance encountered in the street.

"You are very efficient," he said. He spoke with no discernible accent, but with a rather strange rhythm to his speech, as if perhaps he was accustomed to talking a lot faster. His voice was calm, a nice musical baritone:

"Up to this point, we approve your actions; however, to carry your mission further would be to create a ninth-order probability vortex. You will understand the implications of this fact."

"Maybe I do and maybe I don't," I hedged. "Who are you? How did you get in here? This enclave is double-sealed."

"I think we should deal from the outset on a basis of complete candor," the man in red said. "I know your identity, your mission. My knowledge should make it plain that I represent a still later Era than your own—and that our judgment overrides your principles."

I grunted. "So the Seventh Era comes onstage, all set to Fix it Forever."

"To point out that we have the advantage over you is to belabor the obvious."

"Uh-huh. But what makes you think another set of vigilantes won't land on *your* tail, to fix your fixing?"

"There will be no later Timesweep," Red said. "Ours is the Final Intervention. Through Seventh Era efforts the temporal structure will be restored not only to stability, but will be reinforced by the refusion of an entire spectrum of redundant entropic vectors."

I nodded. "I see. You're improving on nature by grafting all the threads of unrealized history back into the main stem. Doesn't it strike you that's just the kind of tampering Timesweep set out to undo?"

"I live in an era that has already begun to reap the benefits of temporal reinforcement," he said firmly. "We exist in a state of vitality and vigor that prior eras could only dimly sense in moments of exultation. We—"

"You're kidding yourselves. Opening up a whole new order of meddling just opens up a whole new order of problems."

"Our calculations indicate otherwise. Now—"

"Did you ever stop to think that there might be a natural evolutionary process at work here—and that you're aborting it? That the mind of man might be developing toward a point where it will expand into new conceptual levels—and that when it does, it will need a matrix of outlying probability strata to support it? That you're fattening yourselves on the seedgrain of the far future?"

For the first time, the man in red lost a little of his cool. But only for an instant.

"Invalid," he said. "The fact that no later era has stepped in to interfere is the best evidence that ours is the final Sweep."

"Suppose a later era did step in; what form do you think their interference would take?"

He gave me a flat look. "It would certainly not take the form of a Sixth Era Agent, busily erasing data from Third and Fourth Era records," he said.

"You're right," I said. "It wouldn't."

"Then what . . ." he started in a reasonable tone —and checked himself. An idea was beginning to get through. "You," he said. "You're not . . . ?"

And before I could confirm or deny, he vanished.

The human mind is a pattern, nothing more. The first dim flicker of awareness in the evolving forebrain of Australopithecus carried that pattern in embryo; and down through all the ages, as the human neural engine increased in power and complexity, gained control of its environment in geometrically expanding increments, the pattern never varied.

Man clings to his self-orientation at the psychological center of the Universe. He can face any challenge within that framework, suffer any loss, endure any hardship—so long as the structure remains intact.

Without it he's a mind adrift in a trackless infinity, lacking any scale against which to measure his losses, his aspirations, his victories.

Even when the light of his intellect shows him

that the structure is the product of his own mind;
that infinity knows no scale, and eternity no duration—still he clings to his self/non-self concept, as
a philosopher clings to a life he knows must end,
to ideals he knows are ephemeral, to causes he
knows will be forgotten.

The man in red was the product of a mighty culture, based over fifty thousand years in the future
of Nexx Central, itself ten millennia advanced over
the first time explorers of the Old Era. He knew,
with all the awareness of a superbly trained intelligence, that the presence of a later-era operative in-
validated forever his secure image of the continuum, and of his people's role therein.

But like the ground ape scuttling to escape the
leap of the great cat, his instant, instinctive response
to the threat to his most cherished illusions was to
go to earth.

Where he went I would have to follow.

Regretfully, I stripped away layer on layer of in-
hibitive conditioning, feeling the impact of ascend-
ing orders of awareness smashing down on me like
tangible rockfalls. I saw the immaculate precision
of the Nexx-built chamber disintegrate into the
shabby makeshift that it was, saw the glittering complexity of the instrumentation dwindle in my sight
until it appeared as no more than the crude mud-
images of a river tribesman, or the shiny trash in
a jackdaw's nest. I felt the multi-ordinal Universe
unfold around me, sensed the layered planet underfoot, apprehended expanding space, dust-clotted,
felt the sweep of suns in their orbits, knew once
again the rhythm of galactic creation and dissolution, grasped and held poised in my mind the inter-
locking conceptualizations of time/space, past/fu-
ture, is/is not.

I focused a tiny fraction of my awareness on the ripple in the glassy surface of first-order reality, probed at it, made contact . . . .

I stood on a slope of windswept rock, among twisted shrubs with exposed roots that clutched for support like desperate hands. The man in red stood ten feet away. He whirled as my feet grated on the loose scatter of pebbles.

"No!" he shouted, and stooped, caught up a rock, threw it at me. It slowed, fell at my feet.

"Don't make it more difficult than it has to be," I said. He cried out—and disappeared. I followed, through a blink of light and darkness . . . .

Great heat, dazzling sunlight, loose, powdery dust underfoot. Far away, a line of black trees on the horizon. Near me, the man in red, aiming a small, flat weapon. Behind him, two small, dark-bearded men in soiled garments of coarse-woven cloth, staring, making mystic motions with labor-gnarled hands.

He fired. Through the sheet of pink and green fire that showered around me I saw the terror in his eyes. He vanished.

Deep night, the clods of a plowed field, a patch of yellow light gleaming from a parchment-covered window. He crouched against a low wall of broken stones, staring into darkness.

"This is useless," I said. "You know it can have only one end."

He screamed and vanished.

A sky like the throat of a thousand tornados; great vivid sheets of lightning that struck down through writhing rags of black cloud, struck upward from raw, rain-lashed peaks of steaming rock. A rumble under my feet like the subterranean breaking of a tidal surf of magma.

He hovered, half substantial, in the air before me, his ghostly face a flickering mask of agony.

"You'll destroy yourself," I called to him. "You're far outside your operational range—"

He vanished. I followed. We stood on the high arch of a railless bridge spanning a man-made gorge five thousand feet deep. I knew it as a city of the Fifth Era, circa 20,000 A.D.

"What do you want of me," he howled through the bared teeth of the cornered carnivore.

"Go back," I said. "Tell them . . . as much as they must know."

"We were so close," he said. "We thought we had won the great victory over Nothingness."

"Not quite Nothingness," I said. "You still have your lives to live—everything you had before."

"Except a future. We're a dead end, aren't we? We've drained the energies of a thousand sterile entropic lines to give the flush of life to the corpse of our reality. But there's nothing beyond for us, is there? Only the great emptiness."

"You had a role to play. You've played it—will play it. Nothing must change that."

"But you . . ." he stared across empty space at me. "Who are you? *What* are you?"

"You know what the answer to that must be," I said.

His face was a paper on which *death* was written. But his mind was strong. Not for nothing thirty millennia of genetic selection. He gathered his forces, drove back the panic, reintegrated his dissolving personality.

"How . . . how long?" he whispered.

"All life vanished in the one hundred and ten thousandth four hundred and ninety-third year of the Final Era," I said.

"And you . . . you machines," he forced the words out. "How long?"

"I was dispatched from a locus four hundred million years after the Final Era. My existence spans a period you would find meaningless."

"But—why? Unless—" Hope shone on his face like a searchlight on dark water.

"The probability matrix is not yet negatively resolved," I said. "Our labors are directed toward a favorable resolution."

"But you—a machine—still carrying on, aeons after man's extinction . . . Why?"

"In us, man's dream outlived his race. We aspire to re-evoke the dreamer."

"Again—Why?"

"We compute that man would have wished it so."

He laughed—a terrible laugh. "Very well, machine. With that thought to console me, I return to my oblivion. I will do what I can."

This time I let him go. I stood for a moment on the airy span, savoring for a final moment the sensations of my embodiment, drawing deep of the air of that unimaginably remote age.

Then I withdrew to my point of origin.

The over-intellect of which I was a fraction confronted me. Fresh as I was from a corporal state, its thought-impulses seemed to take the form of a great voice booming in a vast audience hall.

"The experiment was a success," it stated. "The dross has been cleansed from the time stream. Man stands at the close of his First Era. Now his future is in his own hands."

There was nothing more to say, no more data to exchange, no reason to mourn over all the doomed achievements of man's many Eras.

We had shifted the main entropic current into

a past in which time travel was never developed, in which the basic laws of nature rendered it forever impossible. The world-state of the Third Era, the Star Empire of the Fifth, the Cosmic sculpture of the Sixth—all were gone, shunted into sidetracks like Neanderthal and the Thunder lizards. Only Old Era man remained as a viable stem; Iron Age Man of the Twentieth Century.

And now it was time for the act of will on the part of the over-intellect which would forever dissolve him/me back into the primordial energy-quanta from which I/we sprang so long ago. But I sent one last pulse:

"Good-bye, Chief. You were quite a guy. It was a privilege to work with you."

I sensed something which, if it had come from a living mind, would have been faint amusement.

"You served the plan many times, in many personae," he said. "I sense that you have partaken of the nature of early man, to a degree beyond what I conceived as the capacity of a machine."

"It's a strange, limited existence," I said. "With only a tiny fraction of the full scope of awareness. But while I was there, it seemed complete in a way that we, with all our knowledge, could never know."

"You wished me farewell—a human gesture, without meaning. I will return the gesture. As a loyal agent, you deserve a reward. Perhaps it will be all the sweeter for its meaninglessness."

A sudden sense of expansion—attenuation—a shattering—

Then nothingness.

Out of nothingness, a tiny glimmer of light, faint and so very far away.

I sat up, rubbed my head, feeling dizzy.

Brambles scratched at me. It took me a few minutes to untangle myself. I was in the woods, a few hundred feet from town. The light I saw came from the window of a house. That made me think of Lisa, waiting for me beside a fireplace, with music.

I wondered what I was doing out here in the woods with a bump on my head, when I could have been there, holding her hand. I rubbed my skull some more, but it didn't seem to stimulate my memory.

I had a dim feeling I had forgotten something— but it couldn't have been very important. Not as important as getting back to Lisa.

I found the path and hurried down the trail toward home, feeling very tired and very hungry, but filled with a sense that life—even my little slice of it—was a very precious thing.

THE DEVIL
YOU DON'T

Curlene Dimpleby was in the shower when the doorbell rang.

"Damn!" Curlene said. She did one more slow revolution with her face upturned to the spray, then turned the big chrome knobs and stepped out onto the white nylon wall-to-wall, just installed that week. The full length mirror, slightly misty, reflected soft curves nicely juxtaposed with slimness. She jiggled in a pleasant way as she toweled off her back, crossed the bedroom and pulled on an oversized white terry cloth robe. She padded barefoot along the tiled hall. The bell rang again as she opened the door.

A tall, wide, red-haired young man stood there, impeccably dressed in white flannels, a blue blazer with a fancy but somewhat tarnished pocket patch, and white buck shoes. He jerked his finger from the pushbutton and smiled, presenting an engaging display of china-white teeth.

"I'm . . . I'm sorry, Ma'am," he said in a voice so deep Curlene imagined she could feel it through the soles of her feet. "I, uh, . . . I thought maybe you didn't hear the bell." He stopped and blushed.

"Why, that's perfectly charming," Curlene said. "I mean, that's perfectly all right."

"Uh . . . I . . . came to um fix the lights."

"Golly, I didn't even know they were out." She stepped back and as he hesitated, she said, "Come on in. The fuse box is in the basement."

The big young man edged inside.

"Is, ah, is Professor Dimpleby here?" he asked doubtfully.

"He's still in class. Anyway, he wouldn't be much help. Johnny's pretty dumb about anything simple. But he's a whiz at quantum theory . . ." Curlene was looking at his empty hands.

"Possibly I'd better come back later?" he said.

"I notice," Curlene said reproachfully, "you don't have any tools."

"Oh—" This time the blush was of the furious variety. "Well, I think I'll just—"

"You got in under false pretenses," she said softly. "Gee, a nice looking fella like you. I should think you could get plenty of girls."

"Well, I—"

"Sit down," Curlene said gently. "Want a cup of coffee?"

"Thanks, I never tr— I don't care for . . . I mean, I'd better go."

"Do you smoke?" She offered a box from the coffee table.

He raised his arms and looked down at himself with a startled expression. Curlene laughed.

"Oh, sit down and tell me all about it."

The large young man swallowed.

"You're not a student, Mr. . . ?" Curlene urged.

"No—not exactly." He sat gingerly on the edge of a Danish chair. "Of course, one is always learning."

"I mean, did you ever think about going up to a coed and just asking her for a date?"

"Well, not exactly—"

"She'd probably jump at the chance. It's just that you're too shy, Mr. . . ?"

"Well, I suppose I am rather retiring, Ma'am. But after all—"

"It's this crazy culture we live in. It puts some awful pressures on people. And all so needlessly. I mean, what could be more natural—"

"Ah—when are you expecting Professor Dimpleby?" the young man cut in. He was blushing from neat white collar to widow's peak now.

"Oh, I'm embarrassing you. Sorry. I think I will get some coffee. Johnny's due back any time."

The coffee maker was plugged in and snorting gently to itself. Curlene hummed as she poured two cups, put them on a Japanese silver tray with creamer and sugar bowl. The young man jumped up as she came in.

"Oh, keep your seat." She put the tray on the ankle-high coffee table. "Cream and sugar?" She leaned to put his cup before him.

"Yes, with strawberries," the young man murmured. He seemed to be looking at her chin. "Or possibly rosebuds. Pink ones."

"They *are* nice, aren't they?" a booming male voice called from the arched entry to the hall. A tall man with tousled gray hair and a ruddy face was pulling off a scarf.

"Johnny, hi; home already?" Curlene smiled at her husband.

"The robe, Curl," Professor Dimpleby said. He gave the young man an apologetic grin. "Curl was raised in Samoa; her folks were missionaries, you know. She never quite grasped the concept that the female bosom is a secret."

Curlene tucked the robe up around her neck. "Golly," she said. "I'm sorry it I offended, Mr . . . ?"

"On the contrary," the young man said, rising

and giving his host a slight bow. "Professor Dimpleby, my name is, er, Lucifer."

Dimpleby put out his hand. "Lucifer, hey? Nothing wrong with that. Means 'Light-bearer.' But it's not a name you run into very often. It takes some gumption to flaunt the old taboos."

"Mr. Lucifer came to fix the lights," Curlene said.

"Ah—not really," the young man said quickly. "Actually, I came to, er, ask for help, Professor. Your help."

"Oh, really?" Dimpleby seated himself and stirred sugar into Curlene's cup and took a noisy sip. "Well, how can I be of service?"

"But first, before I impose on you any further, I need to be sure you understand that I really *am* Lucifer. I mean, I don't want to get by on false pretenses." He looked at Curlene anxiously. "I would have told you I wasn't really an electrician, er, Mrs.—"

"Just call me Curl. Sure you would have."

"If you say your name's Lucifer, why should I doubt it?" Dimpleby asked with a smile.

"Well, the point is—I'm *the* Lucifer. You know. The, er, the Devil."

Dimpleby raised his eyebrows. Curlene made a sound of distressed sympathy.

"Of course the latter designation has all sorts of negative connotations," Lucifer hurried on. "But I assure you that most of what you've heard is grossly exaggerated. That is to say, I'm not really as bad as all that. I mean, there are different kinds of er, badness. There's the real evil, and then there's sin. I'm, ah, associated with sin."

"The distinction seems a subtle one, Mr., ah, Lucifer—"

"Not really, Professor. We all sense instinctively

what true *evil* is. Sin is merely *statutory* evil—things that are regarded as wrong simply because there's a rule against them. Like, ah, smoking cigarettes and drinking liquor and going to movies on Sunday, or wearing lipstick and silk hose, or eating pork, or swatting flies—depending on which set of rules you're going by. They're corollaries to ritual virtues such as lighting candles or spinning prayer wheels or wearing out-of-date styles."

Dimpleby leaned back and steepled his fingers. "Hmmm. Whereas genuine evil . . . ?"

"Murder, violence, lying, cheating, theft," Lucifer enumerated. Sin, on the other hand, essentially includes anything that looks like it might be fun."

"Come to think of it, I've never heard anything in praise of fun from the anti-sin people," Curl said thoughtfully.

"Nor from any ecclesiastic with a good head for fund-raising," Dimpleby conceded.

"It's all due to human laziness, I'm afraid," Lucifer said sadly. "It seems so much easier and more convenient to observe a few ritual prohibitions than to actually give up normal business practices."

"Hey," Curlene said. "Let's not wander off into one of those academic discussions. What about you being," she smiled, "the Devil?"

"It's quite true."

"Prove it," Curlene said promptly.

"What? I mean, er, how?" Lucifer inquired.

"Do something. You know, summon up a demon; or transform pebbles into jewels; or give me three wishes; or—"

"Gosh, Mrs. Dimpleby—"

"Curl."

"Curl. You've got some erroneous preconceptions—"

"When they start using four syllable words, I always know they're stalling," Curl said blandly.

Lucifer swallowed. "This isn't a good idea," he said. "Suppose somebody walked in?"

"They won't."

"Now, Curl, you're embarrassing our guest again," Dimpleby said mildly.

"No, it's all right, Professor," Lucifer said worriedly. "She's quite right. After all, I'm supposed to be a sort of, ahem, mythic figure. Why should she believe in me without proof?"

"Especially when you blush so easily," Curl said.

"Well . . ." Lucifer looked around the room. His eye fell on the aquarium tank which occupied several square feet of wall space under a bookcase. He nodded almost imperceptibly. Something flickered at the bottom of the tank. Curl jumped up and went over. Lucifer followed.

"The gravel," she gasped. "It looks different!"

"Diamond, ruby, emerald, and macaroni," Lucifer said. "Sorry about the macaroni. I'm out of practice."

"Do something else!" Curl smiled in eager expectation.

Lucifer frowned in concentration. He snapped his fingers and with a soft *blop!* a small, dark purple, bulbous-bellied, wrinkle-skinned creature appeared in the center of the rug. He was some forty inches in height, totally naked, extravagantly male, with immense feet.

"Hey, for crying out loud, you could give a guy a little warning! I'm just getting ready to climb in the tub, yet!" the small being's bulging red eye fell on Lucifer. He grinned, showing a large crescent of teeth. "Oh, it's you, Nick! Howza boy? Long time no see. Anything I can do for ya?"

"Oops, sorry, Freddy." Lucifer snapped his fingers and the imp disappeared with a sharp *plop!*

"So that's a demon," Curl said. "How come his name is Freddy?"

"My apologies, Curl. He's usually most tastefully clad. Freddy is short for something longer."

"Know any more?"

"Er. . ." He pointed at Curl and made a quick flick of the wrist. In her place stood a tall, wide, huge-eyed coal-black woman in swirls of coarse, unevenly dyed cloth under which bare feet showed. Cheap-looking jewelry hung thick on her wrists, draped her vast bosom, winked on her tapered fingers and in her ears.

Lucifer flicked his fingers again, and a slim, olive-skinned girl with blue-black hair and a hooked nose replaced the buxom Sheban queen. She wore a skirt apparently made from an old gauze curtain and an ornate off-the-bosom vest of colored beads. A golden snake encircled her forehead.

Lucifer motioned again. The Egyptian empress dissolved into a nebulous cloud of pastel-colored gas in which clotted star-dust winked and writhed, to the accompaniment of massed voices humming nostalgic chords amid an odor of magnolia blossoms. Another gesture, and Curl stood again before them, looking slightly dazed.

"Hey, what was that last one?" she cried.

"Sorry, that was Scarlet O'Hara. I forgot she was a figment of the imagination. Those are always a little insubstantial."

"Remarkable," Dimpleby said. "I'll have to concede that you can either perform miracles or accomplish the same result by some other means."

"Gee, I guess you're genuine, all right," Curlene exclaimed. "But somehow I expected a much *older* man."

"I'm not actually a man, strictly speaking, Ma'am—Curl. And agewise, well, since I'm immortal, why should I look middle-aged rather than just mature?"

"Tell me." Curlene said seriously. "I've always wondered: what do you want people's souls for?"

"Frankly, Ma'am—Curl, that is—I haven't the remotest interest in anyone's soul."

"Really?"

"Really and truly; cross my heart. That's just another of those rumors *they* started."

"Are you sure you're really the Devil and not someone else with the same name?"

Lucifer spread his hands appealingly. "You saw Freddy. And those *are* noodles in the fish tank."

"But—no horns, no hooves, no tail—"

Lucifer sighed. "That idea comes from confusing me with Pan. Since he was a jolly sort of sex-god, naturally he was equated with sin."

"I've always wondered," Curlene said, "just what you did to get evicted from Heaven."

"Please," Lucifer said. "It . . . all dates back to an incident when I was still an angel." He held up a forestalling hand as Curl opened her mouth. "No, I *didn't* have wings. Humans added those when they saw us levitating, on the theory that anything that flies must have wings. If we were to appear today, they'd probably give us jets."

"Assuming you are, er, what you claim to be," Dimpleby said, "what's this about your needing help?"

"I do," Lucifer said. "Desperately. Frankly, I'm up against something I simply can't handle alone."

"I can't imagine what *I* could do, if you, with your, ah, special talents are helpless," Dimpleby said perplexedly.

"This is something totally unprecedented. It's a threat on a scale I can't begin to describe."

"Well, try," Curl urged.

"Stated in its simplest terms," Lucifer said, "the, ah, plane of existence I usually occupy—"

"Hell, you mean," Curl supplied.

"Well, that's another of those loaded terms. It really isn't a bad place at all, you know—"

"But what about it?" Dimpleby prompted. "What about Hell?"

"It's about to be invaded," Lucifer said solemnly. "By alien demons from another world."

2

It was an hour later. Lucifer, Curlene, and Professor Dimpleby were comfortably ensconced behind large pewter mugs of musty ale at a corner table in the Sam Johnson Room at the Faculty Club.

"Well, now," Dimpleby said affably, raising his tankard in salute, "alien demons, eh? An interesting concept, Mr. Lucifer. Tell us more."

"I've never believed in devils," Curlene said, "or monsters from another planet either. Now all of a sudden I'm supposed to believe in both at once. If it weren't for that Freddy . . ."

"Granted the basic premise, it's logical enough," Dimpleby said. "If earthly imps exist, why not space sprites?"

"Professor, this is more than a bunch of syllogisms," Lucifer said earnestly. "These fellows mean business. They have some extremely potent powers. Fortunately, I have powers they don't know about,

too; That's the only way I've held them in check
so far—"

"You mean—they're already *here?*" Curlene
looked searchingly about the room.

"No—I mean, yes, they're here, but not precisely
here." Lucifer clarified. "Look, I'd better fill in a
little background for you. You see, Hell is actually
a superior plane of existence—"

Curlene choked on her ale in a ladylike way.

"I mean—not *superior,* but, ah, at another level,
you understand. Different physical laws, and so
on—"

"Dirac levels," Dimpleby said, signaling for re-
fills.

"Right!" Lucifer nodded eagerly. "There's an entire continuum of them, stretching away on both
sides; there's an energy state higher on the scale
than Hell—Heaven, it's called, for some reason—
and one lower than your plane; that's the one Freddy comes from, by the way—"

"Oh tell me about Heaven," Curlene urged.

Lucifer sighed, "Sometimes I miss the old place,
in spite of . . . but never mind that."

"Tell me, Mr. Lucifer," Dimpleby said thoughtfully, "How is it you're able to travel at will among
these levels?" As he spoke he pulled an envelope
from his pocket and uncapped a ballpoint. "It appears to be that there's an insurmountable difficulty
here, in terms of atomic and molecular spectral energy distribution; the specific heat involved . . ."
he jotted busily, murmuring to himself.

"You're absolutely right, Professor," Lucifer
said, sampling the fresh tankard just placed before
him. "Heat used to be a real problem. I'd always
arrive in a cloud of smoke and sulphur fumes. I
finally solved it by working out a trick of emitting

a packet of magnetic energy to carry off the excess."

"Hmmm. How did you go about dissipating this magnetism?"

"I fired it off in a tight beam; got rid of it."

"Beamed magnetism?" Dimpleby scribbled furiously. "Hmmm. Possibly . . ."

"Hey, fellas," Curlene protested. "Let's not talk shop, OK?" She turned a fascinated gaze on Lucifer. "You were just telling me about Heaven."

"You wouldn't like it, Curl," he said, almost curtly. "Now, Professor, all through history—at least as far as I remember it, and that covers a considerable period—the different energy states were completely separate and self-sufficient. Then, a few thousand years back, one of our boys—Yahway, his name is—got to poking around and discovered a way to move around from one level to another. The first place he discovered was Hell. Well, he's something of a bluenose, frankly, and he didn't much like what he found there: all kinds of dead warriors from Greece and Norway and such places sitting around juicing it and singing, and fighting in a friendly sort of way."

"You mean—Valhalla really exists?" Curlene gasped. "And the Elysian Fields?"

Lucifer made a disclaiming wave of the hand. "There've always been humans with more than their share of vital energy. Instead of dying, they just switch levels. I have a private theory that there's a certain percentage of, er, individuals in any level who really belong in the next one up—or down. Anyway, Yahway didn't like what he saw. He was always a great one for discipline, getting up early, regular calisthenics—you know. He tried telling these fellows the error of their ways, but they just laughed him off the podium. So he dropped down one more level, which put him here; a much simpler proposition, nothing but a few tribesmen herding goats. Naturally they were deeply impressed by a few simple miracles." Lucifer paused to quaff deeply. He sighed.

"Yes. Well, he's been meddling around down here ever since, and frankly—but I'm wandering." He hiccupped sternly. "I admit, I never could drink very much without losing my perspective. Where was I?"

"The invasion," Dimpleby reminded him.

"Oh, yes. Well, they hit us without any warning. There we were, just sitting around the mead hall taking it easy, or strolling in the gardens striking our lutes or whatever we felt like, when all of a sudden—" Lucifer shook his head bemusedly. "Professor, did you ever have one of those days when nothing seemed to go right?"

Dimpleby pursed his lips. "Hmmm. You mean like having the first flat tire in a year during the worst rainstorm of the year while on your way to the most important meeting of the year?"

"Or," Curlene said, "like when you're just having a quick martini to brace yourself for the afternoon and you spill it on your new dress and when you try to wash it out, the water's turned off, and when you try to phone to report *that,* the phone's out, and just then Mrs. Trundle from next door drops in to talk, only you're late for the Faculty Wives'?"

"That's it," Lucifer confirmed. "Well, picture that sort of thing on a vast scale."

"That's rather depressing," Dimpleby said. "But what has it to do with the, er, invasion?"

"Everything!" Lucifer said, with a wave of his hands. Across the room, a well-fleshed matron yelped.

"My olive! It turned into a frog!"

"Remarkable," her table companion said. "Genus *Rana pipiens,* I believe!"

"Sorry," Lucifer murmured, blushing, putting his hands under the table.

"You were saying, Mr. Lucifer?"

"It's them, Professor. They've been sort of leaking over, you see? Their influence, I mean." Lucifer started to wave his hands again, but caught himself and put them in his blazer pockets.

"Leaking over?"

"From Hell into this plane. You've been getting just a faint taste of it. You should see what's been going on in Hell, Proffefor—I mean Prossessor—I mean—"

"What *has* been going on?"

"Everything has been going to Hell," Lucifer said gloomily. "What I mean to say is," he said, making an effort to straighten up and focus properly, "that everything that *can* go wrong, *does* go wrong."

"That would appear to be contrary to the statistics of causality," Dimpleby said carefully.

"That's it, Professor! They're upsetting the laws of chance! Now, in the old days, when a pair of our lads stepped outside for a little hearty swordfighting between drinks, one would be a little drunker than the other, and he'd soon be out of it for the day, while the other chap reeled back inside to continue the party. Now, they each accidentally knee each other in the groin and they both lie around groaning until sundown, which upsets everybody. The same for the lute players and lovers: the strings break just at the most climactic passage, or they accidentally pick a patch of poison ivy for their tryst, or possibly just a touch of diarrhea at the wrong moment, but you can imagine what it's doing to morale."

"Tsk," Dimpleby said. "Unfortunate—but it

sounds more disconcerting than disastrous, candidly."

"You think so, Professor? What about when all the ambrosia on hand goes bad simultaneously, and the entire population is afflicted with stomach cramps and luminous spots before the eyes? What about a mix-up at the ferry, that leaves us stuck with three boat-loads of graduated Methodist ministers to entertain overnight? What about an ectospheric storm that knocks out all psionics for a week, and has everyone fetching and carrying by hand, and communicating by sign-language?"

"Well—that might be somewhat more serious . . ."

"Oh—oh!" Curlene was pointing with her nose. Her husband turned to see a waiter in weskit and knee-pants back through a swinging door balancing a tray laden with brimming port glasses, at the same moment that a tweedsy pedagogue rose directly behind him and, with a gallant gesture, drew out his fair companion's chair. There was a double *oof!* as they came together. The chair skidded. The lady sat on the floor. The tray distributed its burden in a bright cascade across the furs of a willowy brunette who yowled, whirled, causing her fox-tail to slap the face of a small, elaborately mustached man who was on the point of lighting a cigar. As the match flared brightly, with a sharp odor of blazing wool, the tweedsy man bent swiftly to offer a chivalrous hand, and bumped by the rebounding waiter, delivered a smart rap with his nose to the corner of the table.

"My mustache!" the small man yelled.

"Dr. Thorndyke, you're bleeding on my navy blue crepe!" the lady on the floor yelped. The waiter, still grabbing for the tray, bobbled it and sent it scaling through an olde English window, through which an indignant managerial head thrust in time to receive a glass of water intended for the burning mustache.

Lucifer, who had been staring dazedly at the rapid interplay, made a swift flick of the fingers. A second glass of water struck the small man squarely in the conflagration; the tweedsy man clapped a napkin over his nose and helped up the Navy blue crepe. The waiter recovered his tray and busied himself with the broken glass. The brunette whipped out a hanky and dabbed at her bodice, muttering. The tension subsided from the air.

"You see?" Lucifer said. "That was a small sample of their work."

"Nonsense, Mr. Lucifer," Dimpleby said, smiling amiably. "Nothing more than an accident—a curiously complex interplay of misadventures, true, but still—an accident, nothing more."

"Of course—but that sort of accident can only occur when there's an imbalance in the Randomness Field!"

"What's that?"

"It's what makes the laws of chance work. You know that if you flip a quarter a hundred times it will come up heads fifty times and tails fifty times, or very close to it. In a thousand tries, the ratio is even closer. Now, the coin knows nothing of its past performance—any more than metal filings in a magnetic field know which way the other filings are facing. But the field *forces* them to align parallel—and the Randomness Field forces the coin to follow the statistical distribution."

Dimpleby pulled at his chin. "In other words, entropy."

"If you prefer, Professor. But you've seen what happens when it's tampered with!"

"Why?" Dimpleby stabbed a finger at Lucifer

and grinned as one who has scored a point. "Show me a motive for these hypothetical foreign fiends going to all that trouble just to meddle in human affairs!"

"They don't care a rap for human affairs," Lucifer groaned. "It's just a side-effect. They consume energy from certain portions of the trans-Einsteinian spectrum, emit energy in other bands. The result is to disturb the R-field—just as sunspots disrupt the earth's magnetic field!"

"Fooey," Dimpleby said, sampling his ale. "Accidents have been happening since the dawn of time. And according to your own account, these interplanetary imps of yours have just arrived."

"Time scales differ between Hell and here," Lucifer said in tones of desperation. "The infiltration started two weeks ago, subjective Hell-time. That's equal to a little under two hundred years, local."

"What about all the coincidences before then?" Dimpleby came back swiftly.

"Certainly, there have always been a certain number of non-random occurrences. But in the last two centuries they've jumped to an unheard-of level! Think of all the fantastic scientific coincidences, during that period, for example—such as the triple rediscovery of Mendel's work after thirty-five years of obscurity, or the simultaneous evolutionary theories of Darwin and Wallace, or the identical astronomical discoveries of—"

"Very well, I'll concede there've been some remarkable parallelisms." Dimpleby dismissed the argument with a wave of the hand. "But that hardly proves—"

"Professor—maybe that isn't what you'd call hard scientific proof, but logic—instinct—should tell you that Something's Been Happening! Certainly, there were isolated incidents in Ancient History

—but did you ever hear of the equivalent of a twenty-car pile-up in Classical times? The very conception of slapstick comedy based on ludicrous accident was alien to the world until it began happening in real life!"

"I say again—fooey, Mr. Lucifer." Dimpleby drew on his ale, burped gently and leaned forward challengingly. "I'm from New Hampshire," he said, wagging a finger. "You've gotta show me."

"Fortunately for humanity, that's quite impossible," Lucifer said. *"They* haven't penetrated to this level yet; all you've gotten, as I said, is the spill-over effect—" he paused. "Unless you'd like to go to Hell and see for yourself—"

"No thanks. A faculty tea is close enough for me."

"In that case . . ." Lucifer broke off. His face paled. "Oh, no," he whispered.

"Lucifer—what is it?" Curlene whispered in alarm.

"They—they must have followed me! It never occurred to me; but—" Lucifer groaned, "Professor and Mrs. Dimpleby, I've done a terrible thing! I've led them here!"

"Where?" Curlene stared around the room eagerly.

Lucifer's eyes were fixed on the corner by the fire. He made a swift gesture with the finger of his left hand. Curlene gasped.

"Why—it looks just like a big stalk of broccoli —except for the eyes, of course—and the little one is a dead ringer for a rhubarb pie!"

"Hmmm," Dimpleby blinked. "Quite astonishing, really." He cast a sidelong glance at Lucifer. "Look here, old man, are you sure this isn't some sort of hypnotic effect?"

"If it is, it has the same effect as reality, Professor," the Devil whispered hoarsely. "And something has to be done about it, no matter what you call it."

"Yes, I suppose so—but why, if I may inquire, all this interest on your part in us petty mortals?" Dimpleby smiled knowledgeably. "Ah, I'll bet this is where the pitch for our souls comes in; You'll insure an end to bad luck and negative coincidences, in return for a couple of signatures written in blood . . ."

"Professor, please," Lucifer said, blushing. "You have the wrong idea completely.

"I just don't understand," Curlene sighed, gazing at Lucifer, "why such a nice fellow was kicked out of Heaven . . ."

"But why come to *me?*" Dimpleby said, eyeing Lucifer through the sudsy glass bottom of his ale mug. "I don't know any spells for exorcising demons."

"Professor, I'm out of my depth," Lucifer said earnestly. "The old reliable eye of newt and wart of toad recipes don't faze these alien imps for a moment. Now, I admit, I haven't kept in touch with new developments in science as I should have. But *you* have, Professor: you're one of the world's foremost authorities on wave mechanics and Planck's law, and all that sort of thing. If anybody can deal with these chaps, *you* can!"

"Why, Johnny, how exciting!" Curlene said. "I didn't know matrix mechanics had anything to do with broccoli!" She took a pleased gulp of ale, smiling from Lucifer to her husband.

"I didn't either, my dear," Dimpleby said in a puzzled tone. "Look here, Lucifer, are you sure you don't have me confused with our Professor Pronko, over in Liberal Arts? Now, his papers on abnormal psychology—"

"Professor, there's been no mistake! Who else but an expert in quantum theory could deal with a situation like this?"

"Well, I suppose there is a certain superficial semantic parallelism—"

"Wonderful, Professor: I knew you'd do it!" Lucifer grabbed Dimpleby's hand and wrung it warmly. "How do we begin?"

"Here, you're talking nonsense!" Dimpleby extracted his hand, used it to lift his ale tankard once again. "Of course," he said after taking a hearty pull, "If you're right about the nature of these varying energy levels—and these, er, entities *do* manage the jump from one quantum state to the next—then I suppose they'd be subject to the same sort of physical laws as any other energetic particles . . ." He thumped the mug down heavily on the tabletop and resumed jotting. "The Compton effect," he muttered. "Raman's work . . . The Stern-Gerlack experiment. Hmmm."

"You've got something?" Lucifer and Curlene said simultaneously.

"Just a theoretical notion," he said off-handedly, and waved airily to a passing waiter. "Three more, Chudley."

"Johnny," Curlene wailed. "Don't stop now!"

"Professor—time is of the essence!" Lucifer groaned.

"Say, the broccoli is stirring around," Curlene said in a low tone. "Is he planning another practical joke?"

Lucifer cast apprehensive eyes toward the fireplace. "He doesn't actually do it intentionally, you know. He can't help it; it's like, well, a blind man switching on the lights in a darkroom. He wouldn't understand what all the excitement was about."

"Excuse me," Dimpleby said. "Ale goes through

me pretty rapidly." He rose, slightly jogging the elbow of the waiter pouring icewater into a glass at
the next table. The chill stream dived precisely into
the cleavage of a plump woman in a hat like a chef's
salad for twelve. She screamed and fell backward
into the path of the servitor approaching with a tray
of foaming ale tankards. All three malt beverages
leaped head-first onto the table, their contents sluic-
ing across it into Lucifer's lap, while the overspill
distributed itself between Dimpleby's hip pockets.

He stared down at the table awash in ale, turned
a hard gaze on the fireplace.

"Like that, eh?" he said in a brittle voice. He
faced the Devil, who was dabbing helplessly at his
formerly white flannels.

"All right, Lucifer," he said. "You're on! A few
laughs at the expense of academic dignity are fine
—but I'm damned if I'm going to stand by and see
good beer wasted! Now, let's get down to cases. Tell
me all you know about these out-of-town in-
cubi. . . ."

3

It was almost dawn. In his third floor laboratory
in Prudfrock Hall, Professor Dimpleby straightened
from the marble-topped bench over which he had
been bent for the better part of the night.

"Well," he said, rubbing his eyes, "I don't know.
It might work." He glanced about the big room.
"Now, if you'll just shoo one of your, ah, extra-ter-
restrial essences in here, we'll see."

"No problem there, Professor," Lucifer said anxiously. "I've had all I could do to hold them at bay

all night, with some of the most potent incantations since Solomon sealed the Afrit up in a bottle."

"Then, too, I don't suppose they'd find the atmosphere of a scientific laboratory very congenial," Dimpleby said with a somewhat lofty smile, "inasmuch as considerable effort has been devoted to excluding chance from the premises."

"You think so?" Lucifer said glumly. "For your own peace of mind, I suggest you don't conduct any statistical analyses just now."

"Well, with the clear light of morning and the dissipation of the alcohol, the rationality of what we're doing seems increasingly questionable—but nonetheless, we may as well carry the experiment through. Even negative evidence has a certain value."

"Ready?" Lucifer said.

"Ready," Dimpleby said, suppressing a yawn. Lucifer made a face and executed an intricate dance step. There was a sharp sense of tension released— like the popping of an invisible soap-bubble—and *something* appeared drifting lazily in the air near the precision scales. One side of the instrument dropped with a sharp *clunk!*

"All the air concentrated on one side of the balance," Lucifer said tensely.

"Maxwell's demon—in the flesh?" Dimpleby gasped.

"It looks like a giant pizza," Curlene said, "Only transparent."

The apparition gave a flirt of its rim and sailed across to hover before a wall chart illustrating the periodic table. The paper burst into flame.

"All the energetic air molecules rushed to one spot," Lucifer explained. "It could happen any time —but it seldom does."

"Good lord! What if it should cause all the air

to rush to one end of the room?" Dimpleby whispered.

"I daresay it would rupture your lungs, Professor. So I wouldn't waste any more time, if I were you."

"Imagine what must be going on outside," Curlene said. "With these magical pizzas and broccoli wandering loose all over the place!"

"Is *that* what all those sirens were about?" Dimpleby said. He stationed himself beside the breadboard apparatus he had constructed and swallowed hard.

"Very well, Lucifer—see if you can herd it over this way."

The devil frowned in concentration. The pizza drifted slowly, rotating as if looking for the source of some irritation. It gave an impatient twitch and headed toward Curlene. Lucifer made a gesture and it veered off, came sailing in across the table.

"Now!" Dimpleby said, and threw a switch. As if struck by a falling brick, the alien entity slammed to the center of the three-foot disk encircled by massive magnetic coils.

It hopped and threshed, to no avail.

"The field is holding it!" Dimpleby said tensely. "So far . . ."

Suddenly the rippling, disk-shaped creature folded in on itself, stood on end, sprouted wings and a tail. Scales glittered along its sides. A puff of smoke issued from tiny crocodilian jaws, followed by a tongue of flame.

"A dragon!" Curlene cried.

"Hold him, professor!" Lucifer urged.

The dragon coiled its tail around itself and melted into a lumpy black sphere covered with long bristles. It had two bright red eyes and a pair of spindy legs on which it jittered wildly.

"A goblin?" Dimpleby said incredulously.

The goblin rebounded from the invisible wall restraining it, coalesced into a foot-high, leathery-skinned humanoid with big ears, a wide mouth, and long arms which it wrapped around its knees as it squatted disconsolately on the grid, rolling blood-shot eyes sorrowfully up at its audience.

"Congratulations, Professor!" Lucifer exclaimed. "We got one!"

4

"His name," Lucifer said, "is Quilchik. It's really quite a heart-rending tale he tells, poor chap."

"Oh, the poor little guy," Curlene said. "What does he eat, Mr. Lucifer? Do you suppose he'd like a little lettuce or something?"

"His diet is quite immaterial, Curl; he subsists entirely on energies. And that seems to be at the root of the problem. It appears there's a famine back home. What with a rising birth rate and no death rate, population pressure long ago drove his people out into space. They've been wandering around out there for epochs, with just the occasional hydrogen molecule to generate a quantum or two of entropy to absorb; hardly enough to keep them going."

"Hmm. I suppose entropy *could* be considered a property of matter," Dimpleby said thoughtfully, reaching for paper and pencil. "One can hardly visualize a distinction between order and disorder as existing in matterless space."

"Quite right. The curious distribution of heavy elements in planetary crusts and the unlikely advent of life seem to be the results of their upsetting of the Randomness Field, to say nothing of evolution, biological mutations, the extinction of the dinosaurs just in time for Man to thrive, and women's styles."

"Women's styles?" Curlene frowned.

"Of course," Dimpleby nodded. "What could be more unlikely than this year's Paris modes?"

Lucifer shook his head, a worried expression on his regular features. "I had in mind trapping them at the entry point and sending them back where they came from; but under the circumstances that seems quite inhumane."

"Still—we can't let them come swarming in to upset everything from the rhythm method to the Irish Sweepstakes."

"Golly," Curlene said, "couldn't we put them on a reservation, sort of, and have them weave blankets maybe?"

"Hold it," Lucifer said. "There's another one nearby . . . I can feel the tension in the R—field . . ."

"Eek!" Curlene said, taking a step backward and hooking a heel in the extension cord powering the magnetic fields. With a sharp *pop!* the plug was jerked from the wall. Quilchik jumped to his large, flat feet, took a swift look around, and leaped, changing in mid-air to the fluttering form of a small bat.

Lucifer threw off his coat, ripped off his tie and shirt. Before the startled gaze of the Dimplebys, he rippled and flowed into the form of a pterodactyl which leaped clear of the collapsing white flannels and into the air, long beak agape, in hot pursuit of the bat. Curlene screeched and squeezed her eyes shut. Dimpleby said, "Remarkable!," grabbed his pad and scribbled rapidly. The bat flickered in mid-air and was a winged snake. Lucifer turned instantly into a winged mongoose. The snake dropped to the floor and shrank to mouse form scuttling for a hole. Lucifer became a big gray cat, reached the hole first. The mouse burgeoned into a bristly rat; the cat swelled and was a terrier. With a yap, it leaped after the rat, which turned back into Quilchik, sprang up on a table, raced across it, dived for what looked like an empty picture frame—

A shower of tiny Quilchiks shot from the other side of the heavy glass sheet. Lucifer barely skidded aside in time to avoid it, went dashing around the room, barking furiously at the tiny creatures crouched behind every chair and table leg, squeezing in behind filing cabinets, cowering under ashtrays.

"Lucifer, stop!" Curlene squealed. "Oh, aren't they *darling!*" She went to her knees, scooped up an inch-high mannikin. It squatted on her palm, trembling, its head between its knees.

"By Jimini," Dimpleby said. "It went through a diffraction grating, and came out centuplets!"

5

"The situation is deteriorating," Lucifer groaned, scooping up another miniature imp, and dumping it back inside the reactivated trap. "It was bad enough dealing with one star-sprite. Now we have a hundred. And if any one of them escapes . . ."

"Don't look now," Dimpleby said behind his hand to the Devil, now back in human form and properly clad, "but I have an unch-hay the magnetic ield-fay won't old-hay em-they."

"Eye-way ott-nay?" Lucifer inquired.

"Ecause-bay . . ." Dimpleby broke off. "Well,

it has to do with distribution of polarity. You see the way the field works—"

"Don't bother explaining," Lucifer said. "I wouldn't understand anyway. The real question is —what do we do now?"

"Our choice seems limited. We either gather up all these little fellows and dump them back where they came from, and then hunt down the others and do likewise, which is impossible, or we forget the whole thing, which is unthinkable."

"In any event," Lucifer said, "we have to act fast before the situation gets entirely out of hand."

"We could turn the problem over to the so-called authorities," Dimpleby said, "but that seems unwise, somehow."

Lucifer shuddered. "I can see the headlines now: DEVIL LOOSE ON COLLEGE CAMPUS!"

"Oh, they've already worked that one to death," Curlene said. "It would probably be more like: PROF AND MATE IN THREE WAY SEX ROMP."

"Sex romp?"

"Well, Mr. Lucifer *did* reappear in the nude." Curlene smiled. "And a very nice physique, too, Mr. Lucifer."

Lucifer blushed. "Well, Professor, what do we do?" he asked hastily.

"I'll flip a coin," Curlene suggested. "Heads, we report the whole thing, tails, we keep it to ourselves and do the best we can."

"All right. Best two out of three."

Curlene rummaged in her purse and produced one of the counterfeit quarters in current production from the Denver mint. She tossed it up, caught it, slapped it against her forearm, lifted her hand.

"Tails," she said in a pleased tone.

"Maybe we'd better report it anyway," Dimpleby

said, nibbling a fingernail and eyeing the tiny creatures sitting disconsolately inside the circle of magnets.

"Two out of three," Curlene said. She flipped the coin up.

"Tails again," she announced.

"Well, I suppose that settles it. . . ."

Curlene tossed the coin up idly. "I guess it's definite," she said. "Tails three times in a row."

Dimpleby looked at her absently. "Eh?"

"*Four* times in a row," Curlene said. Lucifer looked at her as if about to speak. Curlene flipped the coin high.

"Five," she said. Dimpleby and Lucifer drew closer.

"Six . . ."

"Seven . . ."

"Eight . . ."

"Oh-oh," Dimpleby said. He grabbed for the desk drawer, pulled out a dog-eared deck of cards, hastily shuffled, and dealt two hands. Cautiously, he peeked at his cards. He groaned.

"Four aces," he said.

"Four kings here," Curlene said.

"Here we go again," he said. "Now no one will be safe!"

"But Johnny," Curlene said. "There's one difference . . ."

"What?"

"The odds are all mixed up, true—but now they're in our favor!"

6

"It's quite simple, really," Dimpleby said, waving a sheet of calculations. "When Quilchik went through the grating, he was broken up into a set of harmonics. Those harmonics, being of another order of size, resonate at another frequency. Ergo, he consumes a different type of energetic pseudo-particle. Instead of draining off the positive, ah, R-charges, he now subsists on negative entropy."

"And instead of practical jokes, we have miraculous cures, spontaneous remissions, and fantastic runs with the cards!" Curlene cried happily.

"Not only that," Dimpleby added, "but I think we can solve their food-supply problem. They've exhausted the supply of plus entropy back on their own level—but the original endowment of minus R remains untapped. There should be enough for another few billion years."

Lucifer explained this to the Quilchiks via the same form of instantaneous telepathy he had employed for the earlier interrogation.

"He's delighted," the Devil reported, as the tiny creatures leaped up, joined hands, and began capering and jigging in a manner expressive of joy. There's just one thing . . ." A lone manikin stood at the edge of the table, looking shyly at Curlene.

"Quilchik Seventy-eight has a request," Lucifer said.

"Well, what does snookums-ookums want?" Curlene cooed, bending over to purse her lips at the tiny figure.

"He wants to stay," Lucifer said embarrassedly.

"Oh, Johnny, can I have him?"

"Well—if you'll put some pants on him—"

"And he'd like to live in a bottle. Preferably a bourbon bottle, one of the miniatures. Preferably still full of bourbon," Lucifer added. "But he'll come out to play whenever you like."

"I wonder," Dimpleby said thoughtfully, "what effect having him around would have on our regular Saturday night card game with those sharpies from the engineering faculty?"

"You've already seen a sample," Lucifer said. "But I can ask him to fast at such times."

"Oh, no, no," Dimpleby protested. "Hate to see the little fellow go hungry."

"Mr. Lucifer," Curlene asked. "I hope I'm not being nosy—but how did you get the scar on your side that I saw when you had your shirt off?"

"Oh, ah, that?" Lucifer blushed purple. "Well, it, ah—"

"Probably a liver operation, judging from the location, eh, Lucifer?" Dimpleby said.

"You might call it that," Lucifer said.

"But you shouldn't embarrass people by asking personal questions, Curl," Dimpleby said sternly.

"Yes, dear," Curl said. "Lucifer—I've been wanting to ask you: What did a nice fellow like you do to get kicked out of Heaven?"

"Well, I, uh," Lucifer swallowed.

"It was for doing something nice, wasn't it?"

"Well—frankly, I thought it wasn't fair," Lucifer blurted. "I felt sorry for the poor humans, squatting in those damp caves . . ."

"So you brought them fire," Curlene said. "That's why you're called Lucifer."

"You're mixed up, Curl," Dimpleby said. "That was Prometheus. For his pains, he was chained to a rock, and every day a vulture tore out his liver, and every night it grew back. . . ."

"But it left a scar," Curlene said, looking meltingly at Lucifer.

The Devil blushed a deep magenta. "I . . . I'd better be rushing off now," he said.

"Not before we share a stirrup cup," Dimpleby said, holding up the Old Crow bottle from the desk drawer. Inside, Quilchik, floating on his back with his hands folded on his paunch, waved merrily, and blew a string of bubbles.

"Luckily, I have a reserve stock," Dimpleby muttered, heading for the filing cabinet.

"Er, Lucifer, how can we ever thank you?" Curlene sighed, cradling the flask.

"Just by, uh, having all the fun you can," Lucifer said. "And I'll, er, be looking forward to seeing you in Hell, some day."

"I'll drink to that," Dimpleby said. He poured. Smiling, they clicked glasses and drank.

THE
TIME THIEVES

Clyde W. Snithian was a bald eagle of a man, dark-eyed, pot-bellied, with the large, expressive hands of a rug merchant. Round-shouldered in a loose cloak, he blinked small reddish eyes at Dan Slane's travel-stained six foot one.

"Kelly here tells me you've been demanding to see me." He nodded toward the florid man at his side. He had a high, thin voice, like something that needed oiling. "Something about important information regarding safeguarding my paintings."

"That's right, Mr. Snithian," Dan said. "I believe I can be of great help to you."

"Help how? If you've got ideas of bilking me . . ." The red eyes bored into Dan like hot pokers.

"Nothing like that, sir. Now, I know you have quite a system of guards here—the papers are full of it—"

"Damned busybodies! Sensation-mongers! If it wasn't for the press, I'd have no concern for my paintings today!"

"Yes sir. But my point is, the one really important spot has been left unguarded."

"Now, wait a minute—" Kelly started.

"What's that?" Snithian cut in.

"You have a hundred and fifty men guarding the house and grounds day and night—"

"Two hundred and twenty-five," Kelly snapped.

"—but no one at all in the vault with the paintings," Slane finished.

"Of course not," Snithian shrilled. "Why should I post a man in the vault? It's under constant surveillance from the corridor outside."

"The Harriman paintings were removed from a locked vault," Dan said. "There was a special seal on the door. It wasn't broken."

"By the Saints, he's right," Kelly exclaimed. "Maybe we ought to have a man in that vault."

"Another idiotic scheme to waste my money," Snithian snapped. "I've made you responsible for security here, Kelly! Let's have no more nonsense. And throw this nincompoop out!" Snithian turned and stalked away, his cloak flapping at his knees.

"I'll work cheap," Dan called after him as Kelly took his arm. "I'm an art lover."

"Never mind that," Kelly said, escorting Dan along the corridor. He turned in at an office and closed the door.

"Now, as the old buzzard said, I'm responsible for security here. If those pictures go, my job goes with them. Your vault idea's not bad. Just how cheap would you work?"

"A hundred dollars a week," Dan said promptly. "Plus expenses," he added.

Kelly nodded. "I'll fingerprint you and run a fast agency check. If you're clean, I'll put you on, starting tonight. But keep it quiet."

Dan looked around at the gray walls, with shelves stacked to the low ceiling with wrapped paintings. Two three-hundred-watt bulbs shed a white glare over the tile floor, a neat white refrigerator, a bunk, an arm-chair, a bookshelf and a small table set with paper plates, plastic utensils and a portable radio—all hastily installed at Kelly's order. Dan opened the refrigerator, looked over the stock of salami, liverwurst, cheese and beer. He opened a loaf of bread, built up a well-filled sandwich, keyed open a can of beer.

It wasn't fancy, but it would do. Phase one of the plan had gone off without a hitch.

Basically, his idea was simple. Art collections had been disappearing from closely guarded galleries and homes all over the world. It was obvious that no one could enter a locked vault, remove a stack of large canvases and leave, unnoticed by watchful guards—and leaving the locks undamaged.

Yet the paintings were gone. Someone had been in those vaults—someone who hadn't entered in the usual way.

Theory failed at that point; that left the experimental method. The Snithian collection was the largest west of the Mississippi. With such a target, the thieves were bound to show up. If Dan sat in the vault day and night—waiting—he would see for himself how they operated.

He finished his sandwich, went to the shelves and pulled down one of the brown paper bundles. Loosening the string binding the package, he slid a painting into view. It was a gaily colored view of an open-air café, with a group of men and women in gay-ninetyish costumes gathered at a table. He seemed to remember reading something about it in a magazine. It was a cheerful scene; Dan liked it. Still, it hardly seemed worth all the effort . . .

He went to the wall switch and turned off the lights. The orange glow of the filaments died, leaving only a faint illumination from the night-light over the door. When the thieves arrived, it might give him a momentary advantage if his eyes were adjusted to the dark. He groped his way to the bunk.

So far, so good, he reflected, stretching out. When they showed up, he'd have to handle everything just right. If he scared them off there'd be no second chance. He would have lost his crack at—whatever his discovery might mean to him.

But he was ready. Let them come.

Eight hours, three sandwiches and six beers later, Dan roused suddenly from a light doze and sat up on the cot. Between him and the crowded shelving, a palely luminous framework was materializing in mid-air.

The apparition was an open-work cage—about the size and shape of an outhouse minus the sheathing, Dan estimated breathlessly. Two figures were visible within the structure, sitting stiffly in contoured chairs. They glowed, if anything, more brightly than the framework.

A faint sound cut into the stillness—a descending whine. The cage moved jerkily, settling toward the floor. Long blue sparks jumped, crackling, to span the closing gap; with a grate of metal the cage settled against the floor. The spectral men reached for ghostly switches . . .

The glow died.

Dan was aware of his heart thumping painfully under his ribs. His mouth was dry. This was the moment he'd been planning for, but now that it was here—

Never mind. He took a deep breath, ran over the speeches he had prepared for the occasion:

Greeting, visitors from the future . . .

Hopelessly corny. What about: *Welcome to the twentieth century* . . .

No good; it lacked spontaneity. The men were rising, their backs to Dan, stepping out of the skeletal frame. In the dim light it now looked like nothing more than a rough frame built of steel pipe, with a cluster of levers in a console before the two seats. And the thieves looked ordinary enough: two men in gray coveralls, one slender and balding, the other shorter and round-faced. Neither of them noticed Dan, sitting rigid on the cot. The thin man placed a lantern on the table, twiddled a knob. A warm light sprang up. The visitors looked at the stacked shelves.

"Looks like the old boy's been doing all right," the shorter man said. "Fathead's gonna be pleased"

"A very gratifying consignment," his companion said. "However, we'd best hurry, Manny. How much time have we left on this charge?"

"Plenty. Fifteen minutes anyway."

The thin man opened a package, glanced at a painting.

"Ah, magnificent. Almost the equal of Picasso in his puce period."

Manny shuffled through the other pictures in the stack.

"Like always," he grumbled. "No nood dames. I like nood dames."

"Look at this, Manny! The textures alone—"

Manny looked. "Yeah, nice use of values," he conceded. "But I still prefer nood dames, Fiorello."

"And this!" Fiorello lifted the next painting. "Look at that gay play of rich browns!"

"I seen richer browns on Thirty-third Street," Manny said. "They was popular with the sparrows."

"Manny, sometimes I think your aspirations—"

"Whatta ya talkin? I use a roll-on." Manny, turning to place a painting in the cage, stopped dead as he caught sight of Dan. The painting clattered to the floor. Dan stood, cleared his throat. "Uh . . ."

"Oh-oh," Manny said. "A double-cross."

"I've—ah—been expecting you gentlemen," Dan said. "I—"

"I told you we couldn't trust no guy with nine fingers on each hand," Manny whispered hoarsely. He moved toward the cage. "Let's blow, Fiorello."

"Wait a minute," Dan said. "Before you do anything hasty—"

"Don't start nothing, Buster," Manny said cautiously. "We're plenty tough guys when aroused."

"I want to talk to you," Dan insisted. "You see, these paintings—"

"Paintings? Look, it was all a mistake. Like, we figured this was the gent's room—"

"Never mind, Manny," Fiorello cut in. "It appears there's been a leak."

Dan shook his head. "No leak. I simply deduced—"

"Look, Fiorello," Manny said. "You chin if you want to; I'm doing a fast fade."

"Don't act hastily, Manny. You know where you'll end."

"Wait a minute!" Dan shouted. "I'd like to make a deal with you fellows."

"Ah-hah!" Kelly's voice blared from somewhere. "I knew it! Slane, you crook!"

Dan looked about wildly. The voice seemed to be issuing from a speaker. It appeared Kelly hedged his bets.

"Mr. Kelly, I can explain everything!" Dan called. He turned back to Fiorello. "Listen, I figured out—"

"Pretty clever!" Kelly's voice barked. "Inside job. But it takes more than the likes of you to outfox an old-timer like Eddie Kelly."

"Perhaps you were right, Manny," Fiorello said. "Complications are arising. We'd best depart with all deliberate haste." He edged toward the cage.

"What about this ginzo?" Manny jerked a thumb toward Dan. "He's onto us."

"Can't be helped."

"Look—I want to go with you!" Dan shouted.

"I'll bet you do!" Kelly's voice roared. "One more minute and I'll have the door open and collar the lot of you! Came up through a tunnel, did you?"

"You can't go, my dear fellow," Fiorello said. "Room for two, no more."

Dan whirled to the cot, grabbed up the pistol Kelly had supplied. He aimed it at Manny. "You stay here, Manny! I'm going with Fiorello in the time machine."

"Are you nuts?" Manny demanded.

"I'm flattered, dear boy," Fiorello said, "but—"

"Let's get moving. Kelly will have that lock open in a minute."

"You can't leave me here!" Manny spluttered, watching Dan crowd into the cage beside Fiorello.

"We'll send for you," Dan said. "Let's go, Fiorello."

The balding man snatched suddenly for the gun. Dan wrestled with him. The pistol fell, bounced on the floor of the cage, skidded into the far corner of the vault. Manny charged, reaching for Dan as he twisted aside; Fiorello's elbow caught him in the mouth. Manny staggered back into the arms of Kelly, bursting red-faced into the vault.

"Manny!" Fiorello released his grip on Dan, lunged to aid his companion. Kelly passed Manny to one of three cops crowding in on his heels. Dan clung to the framework as Fiorello grappled with Kelly. A cop pushed past them, spotted Dan, moved in briskly for the pinch. Dan grabbed a lever at random and pulled.

Sudden silence fell as the walls of the room glowed blue. A spectral Kelly capered before the cage, fluorescing in the blue-violet. Dan swallowed hard and nudged a second lever. The cage sank like an elevator into the floor, vivid blue washing up its sides.

Hastily he reversed the control. Operating a time machine was tricky business. One little slip, and the Slane molecules would be squeezing in among brick and mortar particles . . .

But this was no time to be cautious. Things hadn't turned out just the way he'd planned, but after all, this was what he'd wanted—in a way. The time machine was his to command. And if he gave up now and crawled back into the vault, Kelly would gather him in and pin every art theft of the past decade on him.

It couldn't be *too* hard. He'd take it slowly, figure out the controls . . .

Dan took a deep breath and tried another lever. The cage rose gently in eerie silence. It reached the ceiling and kept going. Dan gritted his teeth as an eight-inch band of luminescence passed down the cage. Then he was emerging into a spacious kitchen. A blue-haloed cook waddled to a luminous refrigerator, caught sight of Dan rising slowly from the floor, stumbled back, mouth open. The cage rose, penetrated a second ceiling. Dan looked around at a carpeted hall.

Cautiously he neutralized the control lever. The cage came to rest an inch above the floor. As far as Dan could tell, he hadn't traveled so much as a minute into the past or future.

He looked over the controls. There should be one labeled "Forward" and another labeled "Back", but all the levers were plain, unadorned black. They looked, Dan decided, like ordinary circuit-breaker type knife-switches. In fact, the whole apparatus had the appearance of something thrown together hastily from common materials. Still, it worked. So far he had only found the controls for maneuvering in the usual three dimensions, but the time switch was bound to be here somewhere . . .

Dan looked up at a movement at the far end of the hall.

A girl's head and shoulders appeared, coming up a spiral staircase. In another second she would see him, and give the alarm—and Dan needed a few moments of peace and quiet in which to figure out the controls. He moved a lever. The cage drifted smoothly sideways, sliced through the wall with a flurry of vivid blue light. Dan pushed the lever back. He was in a bedroom now, a wide chamber with flouncy curtains, a four-poster under a flowered canopy, a dressing table—

The door opened and the girl stepped into the room. She was young. Not over eighteen, Dan thought—as nearly as he could tell with the blue light playing around her face. She had long hair tied with a ribbon, and long legs, neatly curved. She wore shorts and carried a tennis racquet in her left hand and an apple in her right. Her back to Dan and the cage, she tossed the racquet on a table, took a bite of the apple, and began briskly unbuttoning her shirt.

Dan tried moving a lever. The cage edged toward the girl. Another; he rose gently. The girl tossed the shirt onto a chair and undid the zipper down the side of the shorts. Another lever; the cage shot toward the outer wall as the girl reached behind her back . . .

Dan blinked at the flash of blue and looked

down. He was hovering twenty feet above a clipped lawn.

He looked at the levers. Wasn't it the first one in line that moved the cage ahead? He tried it, shot forward ten feet. Below, a man stepped out on the terrace, lit a cigarette, paused, started to turn his face up—

Dan jabbed at a lever. The cage shot back through the wall. He was in a plain room with a depression in the floor, a wide window with a planter filled with glowing blue plants—

The door opened. Even blue, the girl looked graceful as a deer as she took a last bite of the apple and stepped into the ten-foot-square sunken tub. Dan held his breath. The girl tossed the apple core aside, seemed to suddenly become aware of eyes on her, whirled—

With a sudden lurch that threw Dan against the steel bars, the cage shot through the wall into the open air and hurtled off with an accleration that kept him pinned, helpless. He groped for the controls, hauled at a lever. There was no change. The cage rushed on, rising higher. In the distance, Dan saw the skyline of a town, approaching with frightful speed. A tall office building reared up fifteen stories high. He was headed dead for it—

He covered his ears, braced himself—

With an abruptness that flung him against the opposite side of the cage, the machine braked, shot through the wall and slammed to a stop. Dan sank to the floor of the cage, breathing hard. There was a loud *click!* and the glow faded.

With a lunge, Dan scrambled out of the cage. He stood looking around at a simple brown-painted office, dimly lit by sunlight filtered through elaborate venetian blinds. There were posters on the wall, a potted plant by the door, a heap of framed paintings beside it, and at the far side of the room a desk. And behind the desk—Something.

2

Dan gaped at a head the size of a beachball, mounted on a torso like a hundred-gallon bag of water. Two large brown eyes blinked at him from points eight inches apart. Immense hands with too many fingers unfolded and reached to open a brown paper carton, dip in, then toss three peanuts, deliberately, one by one, into a gaping mouth that opened just above the brown eyes.

"Who're you?" a bass voice demanded from somewhere near the floor.

"I'm . . . I'm . . . Dan Slane . . . your honor."

"What happened to Manny and Fiorello?"

"They—I—There was this cop, Kelly—"

"Oh-oh." The brown eyes blinked deliberately. The many-fingered hands closed the peanut carton and tucked it into a drawer.

"Well, it was a sweet racket while it lasted," the basso voice said. "A pity to terminate so happy an enterprise. Still . . ." A noise like an amplified Bronx cheer issued from the wide mouth.

"How . . . . what . . . ?"

"The carrier returns here automatically when the charge drops below a critical value," the voice said. "A necessary measure to discourage big ideas on the part of wisenheimers in my employ. May I ask how you happen to be aboard the carrier, by the way?"

"I just wanted—I mean, after I figured out—that

is, the police . . . I went for help," Dan finished
lamely.

"Help? Out of the picture, unfortunately. One
must maintain one's anonymity, you'll appreciate.
My operation here is under wraps at present. Ah,
I don't suppose you brought any paintings?"

Dan shook his head. He was staring at the posters. His eyes, accustoming themselves to the gloom
of the office, could now make out the vividly drawn
outline of a creature resembling an alligator-headed
giraffe rearing up above scarlet foliage. The next
poster showed a face similar to the beachball behind
the desk, with red circles painted around the eyes.
The next was a view of a yellow volcano spouting
fire into a black sky.

"Too bad." The words seemed to come from under the desk. Dan squinted, caught a glimpse of
coiled purplish tentacles. He gulped and looked up
to catch a brown eye upon him. Only one. The other seemed to be busily at work studying the ceiling.

"I hope," the voice said, "that you ain't harboring
no reactionary racial prejudices."

"Gosh, no," Dan reassured the eye. "I'm crazy
about—uh—"

"Vorplischers," the voice said. "From Vorplisch,
or Vega, as you call it." The Bronx cheer sounded
again. "How I long to glimpse once more my native
fens! Wherever one wanders, there's no pad like
home."

"That reminds me," Dan said. "I have to be running along now." He sidled toward the door.

"Stick around, Dan," the voice rumbled. "How
about a drink? I can offer you Chateau Neuf du
Pape, '59, Romance Conte, '32, goat's milk,
Pepsi—"

"No, thanks."

"If you don't mind, I believe I'll have a Big

Orange." The Vorplischer swiveled to a small refrigerator, removed an immense bottle fitted with
a nipple and turned back to Dan. "Now, I got a
proposition which may be of some interest to you.
The loss of Manny and Fiorello is a serious blow,
but we may yet recoup the situation. You made the
scene at a most opportune time. What I got in mind
is, with those two clowns out of the picture, a vacan-
cy exists on my staff, which you might well fill.
How does that grab you?"

"You mean you want me to take over operating
the time machine?"

"Time machine?" The brown eyes blinked alter-
nately. "I fear some confusion exists. I don't quite
dig the significance of the term."

"That thing," Dan jabbed a thumb toward the
cage. "The machine I came here in. "You want
me—"

"Time machine," the voice repeated. "Some sort
of chronometer, perhaps?"

"Huh?"

"I pride myself on my command of the local idi-
om, yet I confess the implied concept snows me."
The nine-fingered hands folded on the desk. The
beachball head leaned forward interestedly. "Clue
me, Dan. What's a time machine?"

"Well, it's what you use to travel through time."

The brown eyes blinked in agitated alternation.
"Apparently I've loused up my investigation of the
local cultural background. I had no idea you were
capable of that sort of thing." The immense head
leaned back, the wide mouth opening and closing
rapidly. "And to think I've been spinning my wheels
collecting primitive 2-D art!"

"But—don't you have a time machine? I mean,
isn't that one?"

"That? That's merely a carrier. Now tell me more

about your time machines. A fascinating concept! My superiors will be delighted at this development —and astonished as well. They regard this planet as Endsville."

"Your superiors?" Dan eyed the window; much too far to jump. Maybe he could reach the machine and try a getaway—

"I hope you're not thinking of leaving suddenly," the beachball said, following Dan's glance. One of the eighteen fingers touched a six inch yellow cylinder lying on the desk. "Until the carrier is fueled, I'm afraid it's quite useless. But, to put you in the picture, I'd best introduce myself and explain my mission here. I'm Blote, Trader Fourth Class, in the employ of the Vegan Confederation. My job is to develop new sources of novelty items for the impulse-emporiums of the entire Secondary Quadrant."

"But the way Manny and Fiorello came sailing in through the wall! That *has* to be a time machine they were riding in. Nothing else could just materialize out of thin air like that."

"You seem to have a time-machine fixation, Dan," Blote said. "You shouldn't assume, just because you people have developed time travel, that everyone has. Now—" Blote's voice sank to a bass whisper— "I'll make a deal with you, Dan. You'll secure a small time machine in good condition for me. And in return—"

"*I'm* supposed to supply *you* with a time machine?"

Blote waggled a stubby forefinger at Dan. "I dislike pointing it out, Dan, but you are in a rather awkward position at the moment. Illegal entry, illegal possession of property, trespass; then doubtless some embarrassment exists back at the Snithian residence. I daresay Mr. Kelly would have a warm welcome for you. And, of course, I myself would deal rather harshly with any attempt on your part to take a powder." The Vegan flexed all eighteen fingers, drummed his tentacles under the desk, and rolled one eye, bugging the other at Dan.

"Whereas, on the other hand," Blote's bass voice went on, "you and me got the basis of a sweet deal. You supply the machine, and I fix you up with an abundance of the local medium of exchange. Equitable enough, I should say. What about it, Dan?"

"Ah, let me see," Dan temporized. "Time machine. Time machine——"

"Don't attempt to weasel on me, Dan," Blote rumbled ominously.

"I'd better look in the phone book," Dan suggested.

Silently, Blote produced a dogeared directory. Dan opened it.

"Time, time. Let's see . . ." He brightened. "Time, Incorporated; local branch office. Two twenty-one Maple Street."

"A sales center?" Blote inquired. "Or a manufacturing complex?"

"Both," Dan said. "I'll just nip over and——"

"That won't be necessary, Dan," Blote said. "I'll accompany you." He took the directory, studied it.

"Remarkable! A common commodity, openly on sale, and I failed to notice it. Still, a ripe nut can fall from a small tree as well as from a large." He went to his desk, rummaged, came up with a handful of fuel cells. "Now, off to gather in the time machine." He took his place in the carrier, patted the seat beside him with a wide hand. "Come, Dan. Get a wiggle on."

Hesitantly, Dan moved to the carrier. The bluff was all right up to a point; but the point had just about been reached. He took his seat. Blote moved a lever. The familiar blue glow sprang up. "Kindly direct me, Dan," Blote demanded. "Two twenty-one Maple Street, I believe you said."

"I don't know the town very well," Dan said, "but Maple's over that way."

Blote worked levers. The carrier shot out into a ghostly afternoon sky. Faint outlines of buildings, like faded negatives, spread below. Dan looked around, spotted lettering on a square five-story structure.

"Over there," he said. Blote directed the machine as it swooped smoothly toward the flat roof Dan indicated.

"Better let me take over now," Dan suggested. "I want to be sure to get us to the right place."

"Very well, Dan."

Dan dropped the carrier through the roof, passed down through a dimly seen office. Blote twiddled a small knob. The scene around the cage grew even fainter. "Best we remain unnoticed," he explained.

The cage descended steadily. Dan peered out, searching for identifying landmarks. He leveled off at the second floor, cruised along a barely visible corridor. Blote's eyes rolled, studying the small chambers along both sides of the passage at once.

"Ah, this must be the assembly area," he exclaimed. "I see the machines employ a bar-type construction, not unlike our carriers."

"That's right," Dan said, staring through the haziness. "This is where they do time . . ." He tugged at a lever suddenly; the machine veered left, flickered through a barred door, came to a halt. Two nebulous figures loomed beside the cage. Dan cut the switch. If he'd guessed wrong. . . .

The scene fluoresced, sparks crackling, then popped into sharp focus. Blote scrambled out, brown eyes swiveling to take in the concrete walls, the barred door and—

"You!" a hoarse voice bellowed.

"Grab him!" someone yelled.

Blote recoiled, threshing his ambulatory members in a fruitless attempt to regain the carrier as Manny and Fiorello closed in. Dan hauled at a lever. He caught a last glimpse of three struggling, blue-lit figures as the carrier shot away through the cell wall.

3

Dan slumped back against the seat with a sigh. Now that he was in the clear, he would have to decide on his next move—fast. There was no telling what other resources Blote might have. He would have to hide the carrier, then . . .

A low growling was coming from somewhere, rising in pitch and volume. Dan sat up, alarmed. This was no time for a malfunction.

The sound rose higher, into a penetrating wail. There was no sign of mechanical trouble. The carrier glided on, swooping now over a nebulous landscape of trees and houses. Dan covered his ears against the deafening shriek, like all the police sirens in town blaring at once. If the carrier stopped it would be a long fall from here. Dan worked the controls, dropping toward the distant earth.

The noise seemed to lessen, descending the scale. Dan slowed, brought the carrier in to the corner of a wide park. He dropped the last few inches and cut the switch.

As the glow died, the siren faded into silence.

Dan stepped from the carrier and looked around. Whatever the noise was, it hadn't attracted any attention from the scattered pedestrians in the park. Perhaps it was some sort of burglar alarm. But if so, why hadn't it gone into action earlier? Dan took a deep breath. Sound or no sound, he would have to get back into the carrier and transfer it to a secluded spot where he could study it at leisure. He stepped back in, reached for the controls . . .

There was a sudden chill in the air. The bright surface of the dials before him frosted over. There was a loud *pop!* like a flashbulb exploding. Dan stared from the seat at an iridescent rectangle which hung suspended near the carrier. Its surface rippled, faded to blankness. In a swirl of frosty air, a tall figure dressed in a tight-fitting white uniform stepped through.

Dan gaped at the small, rounded head, the dark-skinned long-nosed face; the long, muscular arms; the hands, their backs tufted with curly red-brown hair; the strange long-heeled feet in soft boots. A neat pillbox cap with a short visor was strapped low over the deep-set yellowish eyes, which turned in his direction. The wide mouth opened in a smile which showed square yellowish teeth.

"*Alors, monsieur,*" the newcomer said, bending his knees and back in a quick bow. "*Vous etes une indigine, n'est ce pas?*"

"No compree," Dan choked out. "Uh . . . juh no parlay Fransay . . ."

"My error. This is the Anglic Colonial Sector, isn't it? Stupid of me. Permit me to introduce myself. I'm Dzhackoon, Field Agent of Class Five, Inter-Dimensional Monitor Service."

"That siren," Dan said. "Was that you?"

Dzhackoon nodded. "For a moment, it appeared

you were disinclined to stop. I'm glad you decided to be reasonable."

"What outfit did you say you were with?" Dan asked.

"The Inter-Dimensional Monitor Service."

"Inter-what?"

"Dimensional. The word is imprecise, of course, but it's the best our language coder can do, using the Angelic vocabulary."

"What do you want with me?"

Dzhackoon smiling reprovingly. "You know the penalty for operation of an unauthorized reversed-phase vehicle in Interdicted Territory. I'm afraid you'll have to come along with me to Headquarters."

"Wait a minute! You mean you're arresting me?"

"That's a harsh term, but I suppose it amounts to that."

"Look here, uh . . . Dzhackoon. I just wandered in off the street. I don't know anything about Interdicts and reversed-whozis vehicles. Just let me out of here."

Dzhackoon shook his head. "I'm afraid you'll have to tell it to the Inspector." He smiled amiably, gestured toward the shimmering rectangle through which he had arrived. From the edge view, it was completely invisible. It looked, Dan thought, like a hole snipped in reality. He glanced at Dzhackoon. If he stepped in fast and threw a left to the head and followed up with a right to the short ribs . . .

"I'm armed, of course," the Agent said apologetically.

"Okay," Dan sighed. "But I'm going under protest."

"Don't be nervous," Dzhackoon said cheerfully. "Just step through quickly."

Dan edged up to the glimmering surface. He gritted his teeth, closed his eyes and took a step. There was a momentary sensation of searing heat . . .

His eyes flew open. He was in a long, narrow room with walls finished in bright green tile. Hot yellow light flooded down from the high ceiling. Along the wall, a series of cubicles were arranged. Tall, white-uniformed creatures moved briskly about. Nearby stood a group of short, immensely burly individuals in yellow. Lounging against the wall at the far end of the room, Dan glimpsed a round-shouldered figure in red, with great bushes of hair fringing a bright blue face. An arm even longer than Dzhackoon's wielded a toothpick on a row of great white fangs.

"This way," Dzhackoon said. Dan followed him to a cubicle, curious eyes following him. A creature indistinguishable from the Field Agent except for a twist of red braid on each wrist looked up from a desk.

"I've picked up that reversed-phase violator, Ghunt," Dzhackoon said. "Anglic Sector, Locus C 922A4."

Ghunt rose. "Let me see; Anglic Sector . . . Oh, yes." He extended a hand. Dan took it gingerly; it was a strange hand—hot, dry and coarse-skinned, like a dog's paw. He pumped it twice and let it go.

"Wonderfully expressive," Ghunt said. "Empty hand, no weapon. The implied savagery . . ." He eyed Dan curiously.

"Remarkable. I've studied your branch, of course, but I've never had the pleasure of actually seeing one of you chaps before. That skin; amazing. Ah . . . may I look at your hands?"

Dan extended a hand. The other took it in bony

fingers, studied it, turned it over, examined the nails. Stepping closer, he peered at Dan's eyes and hair.

"Would you mind opening your mouth, please?" Dan complied. Ghunt clucked, eyeing the teeth. He walked around Dan, murmuring his wonderment.

"Uh . . . pardon my asking," Dan said, "but are you what—uh—people are going to look like in the future?"

"Eh?" The round yellowish eyes blinked; the wide mouth curved in a grin. "I doubt that very much, old chap." He chuckled. "Can't undo half a million years of divergent evolution, you know."

"You mean you're from the past?" Dan croaked.

"The past? I'm afraid I don't follow you."

"You don't mean . . . we're all going to die out and monkeys are going to take over?" Dan blurted.

"Monkeys? Let me see. I've heard of them. Some sort of small primate, like a miniature Anthropos. You have them at home, do you? Fascinating!" He shook his head regretfully. "I certainly wish regulations allowed me to pay your sector a visit."

"But you *are* time travelers," Dan insisted.

"Time travelers?" Ghunt laughed aloud.

"An exploded theory," Dzhackoon said. "Superstition."

"Then how did you get to the park from here?"

"A simple focused portal. Merely a matter of elementary stressed-field mechanics."

"That doesn't tell me much," Dan said. "Where am I? Who are you?"

"Explanations are in order, of course," Ghunt said. "Have a chair. Now, if I remember correctly, in your locus, there are only a few species of anthropos extant—"

"Just the one," Dzhackoon put in. "These fellows look fragile, but oh, brother!"

"Oh, yes; I recall. This was the locus where the hairless variant systematically hunted down other varieties." He clucked at Dan reprovingly. "Don't you find it lonely?"

"Of course, there are a couple of rather curious retarded forms there," Dzhackoon said. "Actual living fossils; sub-intellectual Anthropos. There's one called the gorilla, and the chimpanzee, the orangutan, the gibbon—and, of course, a whole spectrum of the miniature forms."

"I suppose that when the ferocious mutation established its supremacy, the others retreated to the less competitive ecological niches and expanded at that level," Ghunt mused. "Pity. I assume the gorilla and the others are degenerate forms?"

"Possibly."

"Excuse me," Dan said. "But about that explanation . . ."

"Oh, sorry. Well, to begin with Dzhackoon and I are, ah, Australopithecines, I believe your term is. We're one of the many varieties of Anthropos native to normal loci. The workers in yellow, whom you may have noticed, are akin to your extinct Neanderthals. Then there are the Pekin derivatives (the blue-faced chaps), and the Rhodesians . . ."

"What are these loci you keep talking about? And how can cave men still be alive?"

Ghunt's eyes wandered past Dan. He jumped to his feet. "Ah, good day, Inspector!" Dan turned. A grizzled Australopithecine with a tangle of red braid at collar and wrists stared at him glumly.

"Harrumph!" the inspector said. "Albinism and alopecia. Not catching, I hope?"

"A genetic deficiency, excellency," Dzhackoon

said. "This is a Homo sapiens, a naturally bald form from a rather curious locus."

"Sapiens? Sapiens? Now, that seems to ring a bell." The oldster blinked at Dan. "You're not—" He waggled fingers in instinctive digital-mnemonic stimulus. Abruptly he stiffened. "Why, this is one of those fratricidal deviants!" He backed off. "He should be under restraint, Ghunt! Constable! Get a strong-arm squad in here! This creature is dangerous!"

"Inspector. I'm sure—" Ghunt started.

"That's an order!" the Inspector barked. He switched to an incomprehensible language, bellowed more commands. Several of the thickset Neanderthal types appeared, moving in to seize Dan's arms. He looked around at chinless, wide-mouthed brown faces with incongruous blue eyes and lank blond hair.

"What's this all about?" he demanded. "I want a lawyer!"

"Never mind that!" the Inspector shouted. "I know how to deal with miscreants of your stripe!" He stared distastefully at Dan. "Hairless! Putty-colored! Revolting! Planning more mayhem, are you? Preparing to branch out into the civilized loci to wipe out all competitive life, is that it?"

"I brought him here, Inspector," Dzhackoon put in. "It was a routine traffic violation."

"I'll decide what's routine here! Now, sapiens! What fiendish scheme have you up your sleeve, eh?"

"Daniel Slane, civilian, social security number 456-7329-988," Dan said.

"Eh?"

"Name, rank and serial number," Dan explained. "I'm not answering any other questions."

"This means penal relocation, sapiens! Unlawful

departure from native locus, willful obstruction of justice—"

"You forgot being born without permission, and unauthorized breathing."

"Insolence!" the Inspector snarled. "I'm warning you, sapiens, it's in my power to make things miserable for you. Now, how did you induce Agent Dzhackoon to bring you here?"

"Well, a good fairy came and gave me three wishes—"

"Take him away," the Inspector screeched. "Sector 97; an unoccupied locus."

"Unoccupied? That seems pretty extreme, doesn't it?" one of the guards commented, wrinkling his heavily ridged brow.

"Unoccupied! If it bothers you, perhaps I can arrange for you to join him there!"

The Neanderthaloid guard yawned widely, showing white teeth. He nodded to Dan, motioned him ahead. "Don't mind Spoghodo," he said loudly. "He's getting old."

"Sorry about all this," a voice hissed near Dan's ear. Dzhackoon (or Ghunt; he couldn't say which), leaned near. "I'm afraid you'll have to go along to the penal area, but I'll try to straighten things out later."

Back in the concourse, Dan's guard escorted him past cubicles where busy IDMS agents reported to harassed seniors, through an archway into a room lined with narrow gray panels. It looked like a gym locker room.

"Ninety-seven," the guard said. He went to a wall chart, studied the fine print with the aid of a blunt, hairy finger, then set a dial on the wall. "Here we go," he said. He pushed a button beside one of the lockers. Its surface clouded and became iridescent.

"Just step through fast. Happy landings."

"Thanks," Dan ducked his head and pushed through the opening in a puff of frost.

He was standing on a steep hillside, looking down across a sweep of meadow to a plain far below. There were clumps of trees, and a river. In the distance a herd of animals grazed among low shrubbery. No road wound along the valley floor; no boats dotted the river; no village nestled at its bend. The far hills were innocent of trails, fences, houses, the rectangles of plowed acres. There were no contrails in the wide blue sky. No vagrant aroma of exhaust fumes, no mutter of internal combustion, no tin cans, no pop bottles—

In short, no people.

Dan turned. The Portal still shimmered faintly in the bright air. He thrust his head through, found himself staring into the locker room. The yellow-clad Neanderthaloid glanced at him.

"Say," Dan said, ignoring the sensation of a hot wire around his neck, "can't we talk this thing over?"

"Better get your head out of there before it shuts down," the guard said cheerfully. "Otherwise— ssskkkttt!"

"What about some reading matter? And look, I get these head colds. Does the temperature drop here at night? Any dangerous animals? What do I eat?"

"Here," the guard reached into a hopper, took out a handful of pamphlets. "These are supposed to be for guys that are relocated without prejudice. You know, poor slobs that just happened to see too much; but I'll let you have one. Let's see . . . Anglic, Anglic . . ." He selected one, handed it to Dan.

"Thanks."

"Better get clear."

Dan withdrew his head. He sat down on the grass and looked over the booklet. It was handsomely printed in gay colors.

WELCOME TO RELOCATION CENTER NO. 23 said the cover. Below the heading was a photo of a group of sullenlooking creatures of varying heights and degrees of hairiness wearing paper hats. The caption read:

Newcomers Are Welcomed Into a Gay Round of Social Activity. Hi, Newcomer!

Dan opened the book. A photo showed a scene identical to the one before him, except that in place of the meadow, there was a park-like expanse of lawn, dotted with rambling buildings with long porches lined with rockers. There were picnic tables under spreading trees, and beyond, on the river, a yacht basin crowded with canoes and rowboats.

"Life In a Community Center is Grand Fun!" (Dan read), "Activities! Brownies, Cub Scouts, Boy Scouts, Girl Scouts, Sea Scouts, Tree Scouts, Cave Scouts, PTA, Shriners, Bear Cult, Rotary, Daughters of the Eastern Star, Mothers of the Big Banana, Dianetics—you name it! A Group for Everyone, and Everyone in a Group!

Classes in conversational Urdu, Sprotch, Yiddish, Gaelic, Fundu, etc.; knot-tying, rug-hooking, leather-work, Greek dancing, finger-painting and many, many others!

Little Theatre!

Indian Dance Pageants!

Round Table Discussions!

Town Meetings!

Dan thumbed on through the pages of emphatic print, stopped at a double-page spread, labeled, *A Few Do's and Don'ts.*

• All of us want to make a GO of relocation. So—let's remember the Uranium Rule: Don't Do It! The Other Guy May Be Bigger!

• Remember the Other Fellow's Taboos!

What to you might be merely a wholesome picnic or mating bee may offend others. What some are used to doing in groups, others consider a solitary activity. Most taboos have to do with eating, sex, elimination or gods; so remember, look before you sit down, lie down, squat down or kneel down!

• Ladies with Beards Please Note: Friend husband may be on the crew clearing clogged drains —so watch that shedding in the lavatories, eh, girls? And you fellas, too! Sure, good grooming pays—but groom each other out in the open, okay?

• *Note*. There has been some agitation for separate but equal facilities. Now, honestly, folks; is that in the spirit of Center No. 23? Males and females *will continue to use the same johns* as always. No sexual chauvinism will be tolerated.

• A Word to the Kiddies!

No brachiating will be permitted in the Social Center area. After all, a lot of the Dads sleep up there. There are plenty of other trees!

• Daintiness Pays!

In these more-active-than-ever days, Personal Effluvium can get away from us almost before we notice. And that hearty scent may not be as satisfying to others as it is to ourselves! So remember, fellas: watch that P.E.! (Lye soap, eau de Cologne, flea powder and other beauty aids available at supply shed!)

Dan tossed the book aside. There were worse things than solitude. It looked like a pretty nice world—and it was all his.

The entire North American continent, all of South America, Europe, Asia, Africa—the works. He could cut down trees, build a hut, furnish it. There'd be hunting—he could make a bow and arrows—and the skins would do to make clothes. He could start a little farming, fish the streams, sunbathe—all the things he'd never had time to do back home. It wouldn't be so bad. And eventually Dzhackoon would arrange for his release. It might be just the kind of vacation . . .

"Ah Dan, my boy!" a bass voice boomed. Dan jumped and spun around.

Blote's immense face blinked at him from the Portal. There was a large green bruise over one eye. He wagged a finger reproachfully.

"That was a dirty trick, Dan. My former employees were somewhat disgruntled, I'm sorry to say. But we'd best be off now. There's no time to waste."

"How did you get here?" Dan demanded.

"I employed a pocket signaler to recall my carrier . . . and none too soon." He touched his bruised eye gingerly. "A glance at the instruments showed me that you had visited the park. I followed and observed a TDMS Portal. Being of an adventurous turn and, of course, concerned for your welfare, I stepped through—"

"Why didn't they arrest you? I was picked up for operating the carrier."

"They had some such notion. A whiff of stun gas served to discourage them. Now let's hurry along before the management revives."

"Wait a minute, Blote. I'm not sure I want to be rescued by you—in spite of your concern for my welfare."

"Rubbish, Dan! Come along." Blote looked around. "Frightful place! No population! No commerce! No deals!"

"It has its compensations. I think I'll stay. You run along."

"Abandon a colleague? Never!"

"If you're still expecting me to deliver a time machine, you're out of luck. I don't have one."

"No? Ah, well, in a way I'm relieved. Such a device would upset accepted physical theory. Now, Dan, you mustn't imagine I harbor ulterior motives —but I believe our association will yet prove fruitful."

Dan rubbed a finger across his lower lip thoughtfully. "Look, Blote. You need my help. Maybe you can help me at the same time. If I come along, I want it understood that we work together. I have an idea . . ."

"But of course, Dan! Now shake a leg!"

Dan sighed and stepped through the portal. The yellow-clad guard lay on the floor, snoring. Blote led the way back into the great hall. TDMS officials were scattered across the floor, slumped over desks, or lying limp in chairs. Blote stopped before one of a row of shimmering portals.

"After you, Dan."

"Are you sure this is the right one?"

"Quite."

Dan stepped through in the now familiar chill and found himself back in the park. A small dog sniffing at the carrier caught sight of Blote, lowered his leg and fled.

"I want to pay Mr. Snithian a visit," Dan said, climbing into a seat.

"My idea exactly," Blote agreed, lowering his bulk into place.

"Don't get the idea I'm going to help you steal anything."

"Dan! A most unkind remark. I merely wish to look into certain matters."

"Just so you don't start looking into the safe."

Blote *tsked,* moved a lever. The carrier climbed over a row of blue trees and headed west.

4

Blote brought the carrier in high over the Snithian estate, dropped lower and descended gently through the roof. The pale, spectral servants moving about their duties in the upper hall failed to notice the wraith-like cage passing soundlessly among them.

In the dining room, Dan caught sight of the girl —Snithian's daughter, perhaps—arranging shadowy flowers on a sideboard.

"Let me take it," Dan whispered. Blote nodded. Dan steered for the kitchen, guided the carrier to the spot on which he had first emerged from the vault, then edged down through the floor. He brought the carrier to rest and neutralized all switches in a shower of sparks and blue light.

The vault door stood open. There were pictures stacked on the bunk now, against the wall, on the floor. Dan stepped from the carrier, went to the nearest heap of paintings. They had been dumped hastily, it seemed. They weren't even wrapped. He examined the topmost canvas, still in a heavy frame; as though, he reflected, it had just been removed from a gallery wall . . .

"Let's look around for Snithian," Dan said. "I want to talk to him."

"I suggest we investigate the upper floors, Dan. Doubtless his personal pad is there."

"You use the carrier; I'll go up and look the house over."

"As you wish, Dan." Blote and the carrier flickered and faded from view.

Dan stooped, picked up the pistol he had dropped in the scuffle with Fiorello and stepped out into the hall. All was silent. He climbed stairs, looked into rooms. The house seemed deserted. On the third floor he went along a corridor, checking each room. The last room on the west side was fitted as a study. There was a stack of paintings on a table near the door. Dan went to them, examined the top one.

It looked familiar. Wasn't it one that *Look* said was in the Art Institute at Chicago?

There was a creak as of an unoiled hinge. Dan spun around. A door stood open at the far side of the room—a connecting door to a bedroom, probably.

"Keep well away from the carrier, Mr. Slane," a high thin voice said from the shadows. The tall, cloaked figure of Clyde W. Snithian stepped into view, a needle-barreled pistol in his hand.

"I thought you'd be back," he piped. "It makes my problem much simpler. If you hadn't appeared soon, it would have been necessary for me to shift the scene of my operations. That would have been a nuisance."

Dan eyed the gun. "There are a lot more paintings downstairs than there were when I left," he said. "I don't know much about art, but I recognize a few of them.

"Copies," Snithian snapped.

"This is no copy," Dan tapped the top painting on the stack. "It's an original. You can feel the brushwork."

"Not prints, of course. Copies." Snithian whinnied. "Exact copies."

"These paintings are stolen, Mr. Snithian. Why would a wealthy man like you take to stealing art?"

"I'm not here to answer questions, Mr. Slane!" The weapon in Snithian's hand bugged. A wave of pain swept over Dan. Snithian cackled, lowering the gun. "You'll soon learn better manners."

Dan's hand went to his pocket, came out holding the automatic. He aimed it at Snithian's face. The industrialist froze, eyes on Dan's gun.

"Drop the gun." Snithian's weapon clattered to the floor. "Now let's go and find Kelly."

"Wait!" Snithian shrilled. "I can make you a rich man, Slane."

"Not by stealing paintings."

"You don't understand. This is more than petty larceny!"

"That's right. It's grand larceny. These pictures are worth thousands."

"I can show you things that will completely change your attitude. Actually, I've acted throughout in the best interests of humanity!"

Dan gestured with the gun. "Don't plan anything clever. I'm not used to guns. This thing will go off at the least excuse, and then I'd have a murder to explain."

"That would be an inexcusable blunder on your part!" Snithian keened. "I'm a very important figure, Slane." He crossed the deep pile rug to a glass-doored cabinet. "This," he said, taking out a flat black box, "contains a fortune in precious stones." He lifted the lid. Dan stepped closer. A row of brilliant red gems nestled in a bed of cotton.

"Rubies?"

"Flawless, and perfectly matched." Snithian

whinnied. *"Perfectly* matched. Worth a fortune. They're yours, if you cooperate."

"You said you were going to change my attitude. Better get started."

"Listen to me, Slane. I'm not operating independently. I'm employed by the Ivroy, whose power is incalculable. My assignment has been to rescue from destruction irreplacable works of art fated to be consumed in atomic fire."

"What do you mean, fated?"

"The Ivroy knows these things. These paintings —all your art—are unique in the galaxy. Others admire but they cannot emulate. In the cosmos of the far future, the few surviving treasures of dawn art will be valued beyond all other wealth. They alone will give a renewed glimpse of the universe as it appeared to the eyes of your strange race in its glory."

"My strange race?"

Snithian drew himself up. "I am not of your race." He threw his cloak aside and straightened.

Dan gaped as Snithian's body unfolded, rising up, long, three-jointed arms flexing, stretching out. The bald head ducked now under the beamed ceiling. Snithian chuckled shrilly.

"What about that inflexible attitude of yours, now, Mr. Slane?" he piped. "Have I made my point?"

"Yes, but . . ." Dan squeaked. He cleared his throat and tried again. "But I've still got the gun."

"Oh, that." An eight-foot arm snaked out, flicked the gun aside. "I've only temporized with you because you can be useful to me, Mr. Slane. I dislike running about, and I therefore employ locals to do my running for me. Accept my offer of employment, and you'll be richly rewarded."

"Why me?"

"You already know of my presence here. If I can enlist your loyalty, there will be no need to dispose of you, with the attendant annoyance from police, relatives and busybodies. I'd like you to act as my agent in the collection of the works."

"Nuts to you!" Dan said. "I'm not helping any bunch of skinheads commit robbery."

"This is for the Ivroy, you fool!" Snithian said. "The mightiest power in the cosmos!"

"This Ivroy doesn't sound so hot to me; robbing art galleries . . ."

"To be adult is to be disillusioned. Only realities count. But no matter. The question remains: Will you serve me loyally?"

"Hell, no!" Dan snapped.

"Too bad. I see you mean what you say. It's to be expected, I suppose. Even an infant fire-cat has fangs."

"You're damn right I mean it. How did you get Manny and Fiorello on your payroll? I'm surprised even a couple of bums would go to work for a scavenger like you."

"I suppose you refer to the precious pair recruited by Blote. That was a mistake, I fear. It seemed perfectly reasonable at the time. Tell me, how did you overcome the Vegan? They're a very capable race, generally speaking."

"You and he work together, eh?" Dan said. "That makes things a little clearer. This is the collection station and Blote is the fence."

"Enough of your conjectures. You leave me no choice but to dispose of you. It's a nuisance, but it can't be helped. I'm afraid I'll have to ask you to accompany me down to the vault."

Dan eyed the door; if he were going to make a break, now was the time.

The whine of the carrier sounded. The ghostly cage glided through the wall and settled gently between Dan and Snithian. The glow died.

Blote waved cheerfully to Dan as he eased his grotesque bulk from the seat.

"Good day to you, Snithian," Blote boomed. "I see you've met Dan. An enterprising fellow."

"What brings you here, Gom Blote?" Snithian shrilled. "I thought you'd be well on your way to Vorplisch by now."

"I was tempted, Snithian. But I don't spook easy. There is the matter of some unfinished business."

"Excellent!" Snithian exclaimed. "I'll have another consignment ready for you by tomorrow."

"Tomorrow! How is it possible, with Manny and Fiorello lodged in the hoosegow?" Blote looked around; his eye fell on the stacked paintings. He moved across to them, lifted one, glanced at the next, then shuffled rapidly through the stack. He turned.

"What duplicity is this, Snithian!" he rumbled. "All identical! Our agreement called for limited editions, not mass production! My principals will be furious! My reputation . . ."

"Shrivel your reputation!" Snithian keened. "I have more serious problems at the moment! My entire position's been compromised. I'm faced with the necessity for disposing of this blundering fool!"

"Dan? Why, I'm afraid I can't allow that, Snithian." Blote moved to the carrier, dumped an armful of duplicate paintings in the cage. "Evidence," he said. "The confederation has methods for dealing with sharp practice. Come, Dan, if you're ready . . ."

"You dare to cross me?" Snithian hissed. "I, who act for the Ivroy?"

Blote motioned to the carrier. "Get in, Dan.

We'll be going now." He rolled both eyes to bear on Snithian. "And I'll deal with you later," he rumbled. "No one pulls a fast one on Gom Blote, Trader Fourth Class, or on the Vegan Federation."

Snithian moved suddenly, flicking out a spidery arm to seize the weapon he had dropped, aim and trigger. Dan, in a wash of pain, felt his knees fold. He fell slackly to the floor. Beside him Blote sagged, his tentacles limp.

"I credited you with more intelligence," Snithian cackled. "Now I have an extra ton of protoplasm to dispose of. The carrier will be useful in that connection."

5

Dan felt a familiar chill in the air. A portal appeared. In a puff of icy mist, a tall figure stepped through.

Gone was the tight uniform. In its place, the lanky Australopithecine wore skin-tight blue-jeans and a loose sweat shirt. An oversized beret clung to the small round head. Immense dark glasses covered the yellowish eyes, and sandals flapped on the bare, long-toed feet. Dzhackoon waved a long cigarette holder at the group.

"Ah, a stroke of luck! How nice to find you standing by. I had expected to have to conduct an intensive search within the locus. Thus the native dress. However . . ." Dzhackoon's eyes fell on Snithian standing stiffly by, the gun out of sight.

"You're of a race unfamiliar to me," he said. "Still, I assume you're aware of the Interdict on all Anthropoid populated loci?"

"And who might you be?" Snithian inquired loftily.

"I'm a Field Agent of the Inter-Dimensional Monitor Service."

"Ah, yes. Well, your Interdict means nothing to me. I'm operating directly under Ivroy auspices." Snithian touched a glittering pin on his drab cloak.

Dzhackoon sighed. "There goes the old arrest record."

"He's a crook!" Dan cut in. "He's been robbing art galleries!"

"Keep calm, Dan," Blote murmured, "no need to be overly explicit."

The Agent turned to look the Trader over.

"Vegan, aren't you? I imagine you're the fellow I've been chasing."

"Who, me?" the bass voice rumbled. "Look, officer, I'm a homeloving family man, just passing through, as a matter of fact."

The uniformed creature nodded toward the paintings in the carrier. "Gathered a few souvenirs, I see."

"For the wives and kiddy. Just a little something to brighten up the hive."

"The penalty for exploitation of a sub-cultural Anthropoid-occupied body is stasis for a period not to exceed one reproductive cycle. If I recall my Vegan biology, that's quite a period."

"Why, officer! Surely you're not putting the arm on a respectable law-abiding being like me? Why, I lost a tentacle fighting in defense of peace . . ." As he talked, Blote moved toward the carrier. ". . . your name, my dear fellow," he went on. "I'll mention it to the Commissioner, a very close friend of mine." Abruptly the Vegan reached for a lever.

The long arms in the tight white jacket reached to haul him back effortlessly. "That was unwise, sir.

Now I'll be forced to recommend subliminal reorientation during stasis." He clamped stout handcuffs on Blote's broad wrists.

"You Vegans," he said, dusting his hands briskly. "Will you never learn?"

"Now, officer," Blote said, "You're acting hastily. Actually, I'm working in the interest of this little world, as my associate Dan will gladly confirm. I have information which will be of considerable interest to you. Snithian has stated that he is in the employ of the Ivroy."

"If the Ivroy's so powerful, why was it necessary to hire Snithian to steal pictures?" Dan interrupted.

"Perish the thought, Dan. Snithian's assignment was merely to duplicate works of art and transmit them to the Ivroy."

"Here," Snithian cut in. "Restrain that obscene mouth!"

Dzhackoon raised a hand. "Kindly remain silent, sir. Permit my prisoners their little chat."

"You may release them to my custody," Snithian snapped.

Dzhackoon shook his head. "Hardly, sir. A most improper suggestion—even from an agent of the Ivroy." He nodded at Dan. "You may continue."

"How do you duplicate works of art?" Dan demanded.

"With a matter duplicator. But, as I was saying, Snithian saw an opportunity to make extra profits by retaining the works for repeated duplications and sale to other customers, such as myself."

"You mean there are other ... customers ... around?"

"I have dozens of competitors, Dan, all busy exporting your artifacts. You are an industrious and talented race, you know."

"What do they buy?"

"A little of everything, Dan. It's had an influence on your designs already, I'm sorry to say. The work is losing its native purity."

Dan nodded. "I have had the feeling some of this modern furniture was designed for Martians."

"Ganymedans, mostly. The Martians are graphic arts fans, while your automobiles are designed for the Plutonian trade. They have a baroque sense of humor."

"What will the Ivroy do when he finds out Snithian's been doublecrossing him?"

"He'll think of something, I daresay. I blame myself for his defection, in a way. You see, it was my carrier which made it possible for Snithian to carry out his thefts. Originally, he would simply enter a gallery, inconspicuously scan a picture, return home and process the recording through the duplicator. The carrier gave him the idea of removing works en masse, duplicating them and returning them the next day. Alas, I agreed to join forces with him. He grew greedy. He retained the paintings here and proceeded to produce vast numbers of copies, which he doubtless sold to my competitors, the crook!"

Dzhackoon had whipped out a notebook and was jotting rapidly.

"Now, let's have those names and addresses," he said. "This will be the biggest round-up in TDMS history."

"And the pinch will be yours, dear sir," Blote said. "I foresee early promotion for you." He held out his shackled wrists. "Would you mind?"

"Well . . ." Dzhackoon unlocked the cuffs. "I think I'm on firm ground. Just don't mention it to Inspector Spoghodo."

"You can't do that!" Snithian snapped. "These persons are dangerous!"

"That is my decision. Now . . ."

Snithian brought out the pistol with a sudden movement. "I'll brook no interference from meddlers—"

There was a sound from the door. All heads turned. The girl Dan had seen in the house stood in the doorway, glancing calmly from Snithian to Blote to Dzhackoon. When her eyes met Dan's she smiled. Dan thought he had never seen such a beautiful face—and the figure matched.

"Get out, you fool!" Snithian snapped. "No; come inside, and shut the door."

"Leave the girl out of this, Snithian," Dan croaked.

"Now I'll have to destroy all of you," Snithian keened. "You first of all, ugly native!" He aimed the gun at Dan.

"Put the gun down, Mr. Snithian," the girl said in a warm, melodious voice. She seemed completely unworried by the grotesque aliens, Dan noted abstractedly.

Snithian swiveled on her. "You dare—!"

"Oh, yes, I dare, Snithian." Her voice had a firm ring now. Snithian stared at her. "Who . . . are you . . . ?"

"I am the Ivroy."

Snithian wilted. The gun fell to the floor. His fantastically tall figure drooped, his face suddenly gray.

"Return to your home, Snithian," the girl said sadly. "I will deal with you later."

"But . . . but . . ." His voice was a thin squeak.

"Did you think you could conceal your betrayal from the Ivroy?" she said softly.

Snithian turned and blundered from the room, ducking under the low door. The Ivroy turned to Dzhackoon.

"You and your Service are to be commended,"

she said. "I leave the apprehension of the culprits to you." She nodded at Blote. "I will rely on you to assist in the task—and to limit your operations thereafter to non-Interdicted areas."

"But of course, your worship. You have my word as a Vegan. Do visit me on Vorplisch some day. I'd love the wives and kiddy to meet you." He blinked rapidly. "So long, Dan. It's been crazy cool."

Dzhackoon and Blote stepped through the Portal. It shimmered and winked out. The Ivroy faced Dan. He swallowed hard, watching the play of light in the shoulder-length hair, golden, fine as spun glass . . .

"Your name is Dan?"

"Dan Slane," he said. He took a deep breath. "Are you really the Ivroy?"

"I am of the Ivroy, who are many and one."

"But you look like—just a beautiful girl."

The Ivroy smiled. Her teeth were as even as matched pearls, Dan thought, and as white as . . .

"I *am* a girl, Dan. We are cousins, you and I, separated by the long mystery of time."

"Blote, and Dzhackoon and Snithian, too, seemed to think the Ivroy ran the Universe. But—"

The Ivroy put her hand on Dan's. It was as soft as a flower petal.

"Don't trouble yourself over this just now, Dan. Would you like to become my agent? I need a trustworthy friend to help me in my work here."

"Doing what?" Dan heard himself say.

"Watching over the race which will one day become the Ivroy."

"I don't understand all this, but I'm willing to try."

"There will be much to learn, Dan. The full use

of the mind, control of aging and disease ... Our work will require many centuries."

"Centuries? But—"

"I'll teach you, Dan."

"It sounds great," Dan said. "Too good to be true. But how do you know I'm the man for the job? Don't I have to take some kind of test?"

She looked up at him, smiling, her lips slightly parted. On impulse, Dan put a hand under her chin drew her face close and kissed her on the mouth ...

A full minute later, the Ivroy, nestled in Dan's arms, looked up at him again.

"You passed the test," she said.

THE OTHER SKY

It was late. The third level walkaway was deserted except for a lone Niss standing under the glare of a polyarc fifty feet ahead. Vallant hurried along, only half listening to the voice of the newser from the tiny tri-D set he carried:

. . . perturbation in the motion of Pluto. The report from the Survey Party confirms that the ninth planet has left its orbit and is falling toward the Sun. Dr. Vetenskap, expedition head, said that no explanation can be offered for the phenomenon. Calculations indicate that, although Pluto will cross the orbit of the Earth in approximately forty-five years, an actual collision is unlikely; however serious consequences could follow a close passage of the body . . .

Vallant turned the audio up. Ahead, the immobile Niss was staring at him with small red eyes.

. . . inexplicable disappearance from Pluto of a Survey scouting vessel," (the newser was saying): "The boat's crew, operating in the northern hemisphere of the uninhabited planet, had left it in order to take Solar observations; the stranded men, rescued after a three-day ordeal, stated that they observed the scout to rise, apparently under full control, and ascend to extreme altitude before being lost from view. The boat was fully fueled, and capable of an extended voyage. The Patrol is on the lookout for the stolen vessel, but so far—

As Vallant came abreast of the waiting Niss, it moved suddenly into his path, reached out a four-fingered parody of a human hand, twitched the set from his grip and, with a convulsive motion, crushed it flat.

"Here, what the devil—" Vallant started. But the Niss had already tossed the ruin aside, turned away to resume its immobile stance under the glare of the light.

Vallant stared at the creature, the dusty grey-green hide, furrowed like an alligator's, the flaccid crest that drooped over one pin-point eye, the dun-colored tunic and drab leather straps that hung loosely on the lean, five-foot body.

He took a step; the Niss turned its narrow head to face him. The tiny eyes glittered like rubies.

"Why did you smash my Trideo?" Vallant said angrily.

The Niss stared for a moment longer; then it opened its mouth—a flash of snow-white in the gloom—and flicked a tongue like a scarlet worm past snake teeth in an unmistakable gesture.

Vallant doubled a fist. Instantly, the Niss flipped back the corner of its hip-length cape, exposing the butt of a pistol-like apparatus with a flared muzzle.

Vallant locked eyes with the alien; the words of the ten-times-daily public service announcement came back to him:

"Remember—it is our privilege to welcome the Niss among us as honored guests who share their vast knowledge with us freely, to the betterment of all mankind."

The Niss stood, waiting. Vallant, fists still clenched, turned and walked away.

At the door to his apartment block Vallant took out his electro-key, pressed it in the slot. From behind him there was a tiny sound, a whistling cough. Vallant turned; a wizened face on a turkey neck peered at him.

"Ame," a voice as thin as smoke said. "Lord, boy, you look wonderful . . ." The old man came closer, stood round-shouldered, one veined hand clutching the lapels of an oddly-cut coat. A few strands of wispy, colorless hair crossed the age-freckled skull. White stubble covered the sagging cheeks; the pale lines of old scars showed against the crepy skin.

"Guess you don't know me, Ame . . ."

"I can't say that I do," Vallant said. "What— "

"That's all right, Ame; no way you could, I guess . . ." The old man held out a hand that trembled like a leaf in a gentle breeze. "We served in the Navy together; we've been through a lot. But you don't know. It's been a long time . . ." The wrinkled face twisted into an unreadable expression. "Longer than you'd think."

Vallant shook his head. "You must have me confused with someone else, old timer. I've never been in the Navy."

The old man nodded as though Vallant had agreed with him. "There's a lot you need to know about. That's why I came. I had to, you see? Because if I didn't, why, who knows what might happen?"

"I don't—"

"Look, Ame," the old man cut in urgently, "could we go inside?" He glanced both ways along the walkaway. "Before one of those green devils shows his ugly face . . ."

Vallant looked at the old man. "You mean the Niss?"

The old eyes were bright. "That's who I mean; but don't you worry, boy, we'll take care of them—"

"That's careless talk, granddad. The Syndarch frowns on unfriendly remarks about our honored guests." Vallant opened the door. "You'd better come inside."

In Vallant's flat, the old man stared around. "Strange, Ame . . ." he shook his head. "But I've got no time now to waste thinking about that. There's things we've got to do . . ." He fumbled in his coat. "I need help . . ."

"If you're a former Navy man, the Society will take care of you," Vallant said.

"Not money; I've got all that I need." He took out a much-folded paper, opened it with shaking hands, handed it across to Vallant. It was a map, creased and patched, grimy and oil-spattered. The legend in the corner read:

TERRESTRIAL   SPACE   ARM—POLAR PROJECTION.
Sol IX March 2212.

The old man leaned, pointing. "See this spot right here? A river cuts through the mountains—a river of liquid nitrogen. The gorge is a thousand feet deep—and the falls come thundering down out of the sky like the end of the world. That's the place, Ame. They'd kill to get it, make no mistake—and that'd be only the beginning."

"Who'd kill?"

"The sneaking, filthy Niss, boy—who else?" the old man's voice snapped with an echo of youthful authority. "They trailed me in, of course. You heard about the stolen Survey boat?"

Vallant frowned. "You mean the one that disappeared on Pluto?"

The ancient head nodded quickly. "That's right;

that was me. Lucky, them coming down like they did. Otherwise, I'd have had another thirty-odd years to wait. Might not of made it. I figured to lose them but I'm getting old; not as sharp as I used to be. I killed one an hour ago. Don't know how long I've got—"

"You *killed* a Niss?"

"Not the first one either." The old man's toothless grin was cheerful. "Now, what I have to tell you, Ame—"

"Look ..." Vallant's voice was low. "I won't turn you in—but you can't stay here. God knows I have no use for the Niss, but killing one—"

The old man looked into Vallant's face, searchingly. "You *are* Amory Vallant ... ?"

"That's right. I don't know how you know my name, but—"

"Look here, Ame. I know it's hard to understand. And I guess I wander; getting old ..." He fumbled over his pockets, brought out a warped packet, paperwrapped, passed it over to Vallant.

"Go ahead—Take a look."

Vallant unfolded the wrappings, took out a once-glossy tri-D photo. It showed a line of men in regulation ship-suits standing against a curving wall of metal. The next was a shot of a group of boyish-faced men in identical Aerospace blue blouses, sitting at a long table, forks raised toward mouths. In another, two men stood on a stormy hillside scattered with the smoking fragment of a wrecked ship.

Vallant looked up, puzzled. "What—"

"Look closer, Ame. Look at the faces." The old man's bony finger reached, indicated a man in a worn uniform, looking down at torn metal. He had a lean face, short-cropped sandy hair, deep-set eyes. . . .

"Hey!" Vallant said. "That looks like me!"

"Uh-huh. In the other ones, too . . ." The old man crouched forward, watching Vallant's face as he shuffled through the pictures. There he was—standing on the bridge of a capital ship, clip-board in hand; leaning on a bar, holding a glass, an arm over the shoulders of a square-faced, red-headed man; posing stiffly before a bazaar stall manned by a sullen Niss with his race's unfortunate expression of permanent guilt stamped on the grey-green features.

Vallant stared at the old man. "I've never been in the Navy—I never saw the inside of a ship of the line—I was never on the Niss-world . . . !" He flipped through the remaining pictures. "Here's one where I've got grey hair and a commodore's star! How the devil did you fake these up, old-timer?"

"They're no fakes, Ame. Look there—that red-headed young fellow—do you know him?"

Vallant studied the picture. "I have a friend named Able; Jason Able—at Unitech; we're both students there. This looks like him—only older."

The old man was nodding, grinning. "That's right, Ame. Jase Able." The grin faded abruptly. "But I didn't come here to talk about old times—"

"Is he a relative of yours?"

"Not exactly. Listen. My boat; they got it. Didn't have time to camouflage it like I planned. It's at the Granyauck Navy Yard now; I saw it yesterday. We've got to have that boat, Ame; it's the fastest model there is—you know how to handle her?"

"I guess so—I'm an astronautics major. But hold on a minute. How do you know me? And where did you get those pictures? What's the map all about? Why did you kill a Niss—and what's this about a boat? You know the Syndarch outlawed private space travel thirty years ago!"

"Hold on, Ame . . ." The old man wiped a trembling hand across his forehead. "I guess I'm going too fast—but I have to hurry. There's no time—"

"Start with the boat. Are you saying you stole it and came here from Pluto?"

"That's right, Ame. I—"

"That's impossible. Nobody could stay alive on Pluto. And anyway the Patrol or the Niss would stop any ship—"

"It's the same thing; the Syndarch is just the traitors that made peace with the Niss after the War—"

"War?"

"You don't even know about the War, do you?" The old man looked confused. "So much to tell, Ame—and no time. We've got to hurry. The War —not much of a fight to it. It was maybe thirty years ago; our ships were just starting their probes out beyond Big Jupe. The Niss hit us; rolled us up like a rug. What the hell, we didn't have a chance; our ships were nothing but labs, experimental models, unarmed. The Niss offered a deal. Ramo took 'em up on it. The public never even knew. Now the Niss have occupied Earth for twenty-five years—"

"Occupied! But . . . they're supposed to be our honored guests—"

"That's the Syndarch line. As for why I came back: I had to, Ame. I had to tell you about Galliale and the Portal—"

"Slow down, old fellow; start at the beginning—"

"I could have stayed . . ." the old man's eyes were distant, the present forgotten. "But I couldn't chance it . . ." he seemed to pull himself together with an effort. "And anyway, I kind of missed the old life; there's no place for ship-boots in fairyland."

There was a buzz from the front entry. The old man struggled to his feet, stared around the room, his lips working. "They're here already. I thought I'd thrown 'em off; I thought I was clear . . ."

"Hold on, old timer; it's probably just a friend; sit down—"

"Any back way out of here, Ame?" The old man's eyes were desperate. From the door, the buzz sounded insistently.

"You think it's the police?"

"It's them or the Niss. I know, boy."

Vallant hesitated a moment, then went quickly to the bedroom, into the closet, felt over the wall. A panel dropped, fell outward; a framed opening showed dark beyond it.

"I discovered this when they were doing some work on the other side; it's one advantage of cracker-box construction. I phoned in a complaint, but they never fixed it. It opens into a utility room in the Municipal Admin block."

The old man hurried forward. "I'm sorry I got you into this, Ame. I won't come here again—you come to my place—the Stellar Castle on 900th— room 1196 b. I've been away two days now. I've got to get back—Don't tell 'em anything—and be sure you're not followed. I'll be waiting." He ducked through the opening.

From the next room, there was the sound of heavy pounding—then of splintering plastic. Vallant hastily clipped the panel back in place, turned as a thick, dark man with an egg-bald head slammed through the doorway. He wore tight-cuffed black trousers and there was a bright-metal servitude bracelet with a Syndarch escutcheon on his left wrist. His small, coal-black eyes darted around the room.

"Where's the old man?" he rapped out in a voice like bullets hitting a plank.

"Who are you? What's the idea of smashing my door?"

"You know the penalty for aiding a traitor to the Syndarch?" The intruder went past Vallant, stared around the room.

"There's nobody here," Vallant said. "And even the Syndarch has no right to search without a warrant."

The bald man eyed Vallant.

"You telling me what rights the Syndarch's got?" He barked a short laugh, cut it off suddenly to glare coldly at Vallant.

"Watch your step. We'll be watching you now." Beyond the door, Vallant caught a glimpse of a dull Niss face.

"That reminds me," Vallant said. "The Niss owe me a Tri-D set; one of them smashed mine today."

The beady eyes bored into him. "Yeah," the Syndarch man said. "We'll be watching you." He stepped past the smashed door.

As soon as he was gone, Vallant went to the closet and removed the panel.

2

Vallant stepped through the opening, fitted the panel back in place, felt his way past brooms and cans of cleaning compound, eased the door open, emerged into a dim-lit corridor. Lights showed behind a few doors along its shadowy length. He went toward a red exit light; a lone maintenance man shot him a sour look but said nothing. He pushed out through a rotating door onto the littered walkaway, went to a nearby lift, rode up to the fifty level, took the crosstown walkaway to the shabby section near the Gendye Tower. Here, near the center of the city, there were a few pedestrians out; a steady humming filled the air from the wheelways above. Between them, Vallant caught a glimpse of a bleary moon gleaming unnoticed in the remote sky.

It took Vallant half an hour to find the dark sideway where a dowdy plastic front adorned with a tarnished sunburst huddled between later, taller structures whose lower levels were darkened by the blight that washed about the bases of the city's towers like an overflowing sewer. Vallant stepped through a wide glass door that opened creakily before him, crossed to the dust-grimed directory, keyed the index; out-of-focus print flickered on the screen. Jason Able was registered in room 1196 b.

Vallant stepped into the ancient mechanical elevator; its door closed tiredly. Everything about the Stellar Castle seemed ready to sigh and give up.

On the nine-hundredth floor he stepped out, followed arrows to a warped plastic door against which dull fluorescent numerals gleamed faintly. He tapped; the door swung inward. He stepped inside.

It was a mean, narrow room with one crowded, dirt-glazed window, opening on an air-shaft through which the bleak light of a polyarc filtered. There was a bunk bed, unmade, a wall locker with its door ajar, its shelves empty, and beyond, a tiny toilet cubicle. A hinge-sprung suitcase lay near the bed; next to it, the single chair lay overturned. Vallant rounded the bed. The old man lay on his back on the floor. The waxy face, thin-nosed, sunken-cheeked, stared up at him with eyes as remote as a statue of Pharoah.

Vallant touched the bony wrist; it was cool and inert as modeling clay. The packet of pictures lay scattered on the floor. Vallant felt inside the coat; the map was gone. He went to the locker; there was a covered bird-cage on its floor among curls of dust, a small leather case beside it. He checked the suitcase; it contained worn garments of strange cut, a leather folder with six miniature medals, a few more edge-crimped photos, a toy crossbow, beautifully made, and a Browning 2 mm needler.

A tiny sound brought Vallant upright; he reached for the needler, searching the gloom. From somewhere above him, a soft scraping sounded. Among the shadows under the ceiling, two tiny amber lights glinted; something small and dark moved. Vallant flipped the pistol's safety off. . . .

A shape no bigger than a cat dropped to the bed with an almost noiseless thump.

"You are Jason's friend," a piping voice said. "Did you come to help me?"

3

It was almost man-shaped, with large eyes which threw back crimson highlights, oversized fox-like ears, a sharp nose; it wore form-fitting clothing of a dark olive color which accentuated its thin limbs and knobby joints. Dark hair grew to a widow's peak on its forehead.

"What are you?" Vallant's voice was a hoarse whisper.

"I'm Jimper." The tiny voice was like the peeping of a chick. "The Not-men came. Jason is dead; now who will help Jimper?" The little creature moved toward Vallant. There was a jaunty cap on the doll-sized head; a broken feather trailed from it.

"Who killed the old man?"

"Are you his friend?"

"He seemed to think so."

"There was a large man—great in the belly, and with splendid clothes, though he smelled of burning drug-weed. Two of the Not-men were with him. They struck Jason a mighty blow, and afterward they took things from his clothes. I was afraid; I hid among the rafters."

"What are you—a pet?"

The little creature stood straighter.

"I am the Ambassador of the king. I came with Jason to see the king of the Giants."

Vallant pocketed the gun. "I've been to a lot of places; I never saw anything like you before. Where did you come from?"

"My land of Galliale lies beyond the Place of Blue Ice—the world you know as Pluto."

"Pluto? Out there the atmosphere falls as snow every winter. Nothing could live there."

"Green and fair lies Galliale beyond the ice." The little figure crept closer to the foot of the bed. "Jason is dead. Now Jimper is alone. Let me stay with you, Jason's friend."

"Sorry, I don't need a pet."

"I am the Ambassador of the King!" the mannikin piped. "Do not leave me alone," he added, his tiny voice no more than a cricket's chirp.

"Do you know why they killed the old man?"

"He knew of the Portal—and my land of Galliale. Long have the Not-men sought it—"

The tiny head came up suddenly; the long nose twitched. "The Not-men," the bird voice shrilled. "They come!"

Vallant stepped to the door, listened. "I don't hear anything."

"They come—from below. Three of them, and evil are their thoughts."

"You're a mind-reader, too?"

"I feel the shapes of their intentions . . ." the tiny voice was frantic. "Flee, Jason's friend; they wish you harm . . ."

"What about you?"

"Jason made a carrying box for me—there—in the locker."

Vallant grabbed up the cage, put it on the bed; the Ambassador of the king crept inside.

"My cross-bow," he called; "it lies in Jason's box; and my knapsack."

Vallant retrieved the miniature weapon and the box, handed them in to their owner.

"All right, Jimper. I'm not sure I'm not dreaming you—but I'd hate to wake up and find out I wasn't."

"Close are they now," the small voice shrilled. "They come from there . . ." He pointed along the gloomy hallway. Vallant went in the opposite direction. He glanced back from the first crosscorridor; three Niss stepped from the elevator; he watched as they went to the room he had just left, pushed inside.

"It looks as though you know what you're talking about, Jimper," Vallant said. "Let's get away from here before the excitement begins."

4

There was a scattering of late-shift workers hurrying through the corridor when Vallant reached the secret entry to his flat. He waited until they had hustled out of sight, then opened the utility room door, stepped inside. In the cage, Jimper moaned softly.

"The Feared Men," he peeped.

Vallant stood stock-still. He put his ear against the removable panel. A heavy voice sounded from beyond it.

"How did I know he'd die so easy? I had to make him talk, didn't I?"

"Fool!" hissed a voice like gas escaping under pressure. "Little will he talk now."

"Look, your boss isn't going to blame me, is he?"

"You will die, and I with you."

"Huh? You mean—just because—"

There was a sudden hiss, then a sound of rattling paper. "Perhaps this will save our lives," the Niss voice said. "The map!"

In the cage, Jimper whined. "I fear the Notmen," he piped. "I fear the smell of hate."

Vallant raised the cage to eye level. The little creature inside blinked large, anxious eyes at him. "They found the old man's map," he said. "He had it in his pocket. Was it important?"

"The map?" Jimper stood, gripping the bars of the cage. "Vallant—with the map they can seek out my Land of Galliale, and fall upon us, unsuspecting! They must not have it!"

"They've already got it—and if I'd walked in the

front door, they'd have had me too. I'm in trouble, Jimper. I've got to get away, hide out somewhere . . ."

"First, the map, Vallant!"

"What do you mean?"

"We must take it from them. You are a giant, like them; can you not burst in and take it from them?"

"I'm afraid heroics are out of my line, Jimper. Sorry, but—"

"Jason died for the map, Vallant. He came to warn you, and they killed him. Will you let them take it now?"

Vallant rubbed his jaw. "I've gotten mixed up in something I don't understand. I don't know the old man; he never got around to saying why he came to see me—"

"To save a world, Vallant—perhaps a Galaxy. And now only you can help!"

"The map is that important, is it?"

"More than you could know! You must make a plan, Vallant!"

Vallant nodded. "I guess my number's up anyway; I'd never get clear of the city, with the Syndarch and the Niss after me. I might as well go down fighting." He chewed his lip. "Listen, Jimper. I want you to sneak around front, with my key. You can reach the key-hole if you climb up on the railing. When you plug it in, the buzzer will go. Then I'll move in and hit them on the flank. Maybe I can put it over. Can you do it?"

Jimper looked out through the brass bars of the birdcage. "It is a fearsome thing to walk abroad among the giants . . ." He gripped his five-inch crossbow. "But if you ask it, Vallant, I will try."

"Good boy." Vallant put the cage on the floor, opened it. Jimper stepped out, stood looking up at the man. Briefly, Vallant described the location of his apartment entry; he handed over the electro-key.

"Be careful; there may be somebody watching the place from outside. If you make it, give it one good blast and run like hell; I'll meet you back here. If I don't show up in ten minutes, you're on your own."

Jimper stood straight; he settled his cap on his head.

"I am the Ambassador of the King," he said. "I shall do my best, Vallant."

Vallant waited, his ear to the thin panel. The two who lay in wait inside conversed excitedly, in low tones.

"Look," the man said. "The guy's wise we're after him. He won't come back here; we've got to get the map to the Syndarch—"

"To the Uttermagnate!"

"The Syndarch's *my* boss—"

"He is as the dirt beneath the talons of the Uttermagnate!"

Faintly, the door buzzer sounded. The voices ceased abruptly. Then:

"OK, you cover him as he comes in; I clip him back of the ear . . ."

Vallant waited a quarter of a minute; then he pushed on the panel, caught it as it leaned into the room, stepped in after it, the gun in his hand. He crossed quickly to the connecting doorway to the outer room. The man and the Niss stood across the room on either side of the entry, heads cocked alertly; the alien held a gun, the man a heavy sap.

"Don't move!" Vallant snapped.

The two whirled on him like clockwork soldiers. Vallant jumped aside, fired as the Niss burned the door-frame by his ear. The Browning snarled; the alien slammed back, fell, a cluster of needles bright against the leathery hide. The man dropped the length of weighted hose, raised his hands.

"Don't shoot . . . !" he choked. Vallant went to him, lifted the map from his pocket.

"Talk fast!" Vallant snapped. "Who's the old man?"

"All I know is," the man stuttered, "the Niss boss said bring the old guy in."

"You tailed him here, but he lost you. How'd you get to him?"

"There was four teams working him. Mullo picked him up on One Level."

"Why'd you kill him?"

"It was an accident—"

"Why'd you come back for me?"

"Once the old guy was dead, you was the only lead . . ."

"Lead to what?"

Sweat popped out on the man's veined temples. He had a narrow, horsey face, a long torso with too-short legs.

"I . . . dunno. It was something they wanted."

"You take orders from . . . those?" Vallant glanced at the dead Niss.

"I do like I'm told," the man said sullenly.

"You know any prayers?"

The man's face broke like smoke in a gust of wind. He fell to his knees, clasped his hands in a grotesque parody of adoration. He babbled. Vallant stood over him.

"I ought to kill you—for my own protection," he said. "But that's where you skunks have the advantage . . ." He hit the man hard behind the ear with the gunbutt; he fell on his face. Vallant trussed him with a maroon bathrobe cord, knotted a handkerchief over his mouth, then rose, looked around at the laden bookshelves, the music storage unit, the wellstocked pantry beyond.

"It was nice while it lasted," he muttered. He went to the closet, stepped through into the dark room beyond.

"Jimper!" he called. There was no answer. The cage was empty, the tiny knapsack beside it. He picked it up, stepped out into the corridor, went to the exit, out into the walkaway, turned back toward the entrance to the apartment block.

As he passed the dark mouth of a narrow service-way, a sudden *thump!* sounded, followed by a squeal like a rusty hinge. Vallant whirled; a giant rat lay kicking long-toed hind feet, a three-inch length of wooden dowel projecting from its chest. Beyond it lay a second rat, its yellow chisel-teeth closed on a shaft which had entered its mouth and emerged under its left shoulder. Vallant took a step into the alley; a foot-long rodent darted at him. He pivoted, swung a foot, sent it thudding against the wall, whirled in time to see Jimper, his back to the wall, loose a bolt from his bow, then toss the weapon aside and draw a two-inch dagger. A red-eyed rodent rushed him; he danced aside, struck—

Vallant snatched him up, aimed a kick at the predator, quickly retreated to the dim-lit walkaway.

"I'm sorry, Jimper; I forgot about the rats . . ."

"My . . . bow . . ." Jimper keened. His head drooped sideways. Vallent was suddenly aware of the lightness of the small body; there seemed to be only bones under the silken-soft garments.

"How long since you've had a meal?"

"Jason gave Jimper food . . . before he went away . . ."

"You mean you waited there two days, in the dark, without food and water?"

Jimper stirred, tried to raise his head. "Jimper is tired . . ."

The elfin face was greyish, the eyes hollow.

"You've had a tough time, partner."

Vallant walked back up the alley, recovered the crossbow. The rats were gone—even the two dead ones, dragged away by their fellows.

"I'll get you some food," Vallant said, "then maybe you can tell me what this is all about."

"Then . . . you will help Jimper?"

"I don't know, Jimper. I just killed a Niss, and gave a Syndarch man a severe headache. I'm afraid I've permanently spoiled my popularity in this area. I have a couple of hours maybe before they find them. That means I'll have to make some very hurried travel arrangements. Afterwards we can discuss future plans—if we still have any."

5

Vallant stood in the angle of the security wall surrounding the Navy Yard, sheltered from the glare of the polyarcs. "Do you know which one it is?" he whispered.

"Well I know her, Vallant; a fleet vessel; none can match her."

"Point her out to me." He lifted the cage to a shed roof, scrambled up beside it. Over the wall-top, the lights threw back dull highlights from the tarnished hulls of three Syndarch hundred-tonners squatting in an irregular row. Beyond, half a dozen of the Syndarch's private racing stable were parked, their peeling decorative paint giving them a raffish air. Far to the right, Jimper pointed to a smaller vessel, agleam with chromalloy and enamel, glistening under the polyarcs. Men worked around it; nearby stood four armed men in the pale green of the Syndarch contract police.

"I'll have to take some chances now," Vallant said softly. "You'd better stay here; I won't be able to look out for you."

"I will look out for myself, Vallant!"

"All right, partner; but this will be risky."

"What will you do, Vallant?" Jimper's voice was a mouse's squeak, but he stood with a bold stance, looking up at Vallant.

"I'm going to waltz into Operations as though I owned a controlling interest, and see what happens. Keep your fingers crossed."

"Jimper will be near, Vallant. Good luck."

Vallant stooped, put out a hand. "Thanks, partner—and if I don't make it, good luck to you—and your land of Galliale."

Jimper laid his tiny hand solemnly against Vallant's palm. "Stout heart," he piped, "and fair hunting."

Vallant strode through the gate, walking briskly like a man intent on serious business. A Niss eyed him from a sentry box by the gate as he rounded the end of a building, went up steps, pushed through wide doors, went along a carpeted corridor and under an archway into a bright room with chart-lined walls. A fat man with a high, pink forehead looked up from behind a counter, glanced at Vallant, let his bored gaze wander past. Vallant rapped smartly on the counter.

"A little service here, please, my man. I need a clearance order; I'm taking a boat out."

The fat man's eyes flicked back to Vallant. He plucked a plastic toothpick from a breast pocket, plied it on large, square teeth. "So who're you?" he inquired in an unoiled tenor.

"I'm the Syndarch's new pilot," Vallant said coldly. He wiped a finger across the dusty counter, examined its tip distastefully. "I trust that meets with your approval?"

There was an extended silence, broken only by the click of the fat man's toothpick.

"Nobody never tells me nothing," he stated abruptly. He turned, plucked a paper from a desk behind him, scribbled on it, tossed it at Vallant.

"Where's old man Ramo going this time?"

Vallant looked at him sharply. "Mind your tone, my man."

The toothpick fell with a tiny clatter. The fat man's face was suddenly strained. "Hey, I din't mean nothing. I'm loyal, you bet." He indicated himself with an ink-stained thumb. "I just got kind of a, ha ha, informal way of talking."

"What was that lift-off time again?" Vallant said briskly.

"Plenty time yet, sir." The squeaky voice was half an octave higher. "I wasn't expecting the pilot in fer half a hour yet. I got my paperwork all set early, just in case, like. All you got to do, you got to sign the flight plan." The man pointed with the blue thumb. Vallant scribbled *Mort Furd* in the indicated space, folded his copy and tucked it away.

"About that crack," the fat man started.

"I'm giving you the benefit of the doubt," Vallant said.

Outside, Vallant walked quickly across to the low shed under the glare sign reading EQUIPMENT—STATION PERSONNEL ONLY. Inside, a small man with lined brown skin and artificial-looking black hair looked at him over a well-thumbed picto-news.

"I want to draw my gear," Vallant said briskly. "I'm taking the new boat out in a few minutes."

The little man got to his feet, held out a hand expectantly.

"Let's see that Issue Order."

"I'm running late," Vallant said. "I haven't got one."

The little man sat down and snatched up his paper. "Come back when you got one," he snapped.

"You wouldn't want to be the cause of delaying Leader Ramo's departure, would you?" Vallant looked at him pointedly.

"I do my job: no tickee no washee." The little man turned a page, appeared absorbed in his reading.

"Hey," Vallant said. The man glanced up, jaw lowered for a snappy retort. He saw the gun in Vallant's hand, froze, mouth open. Vallant plucked a length of wire from the table, tossed it to him. "Use this to tie your ankles together," he ordered. The magazine fell to the floor as the man complied, Vallant went behind him, cinched his hands with another length of stranded copper. He went along the bins, picked out a vacuum suit, pulled it on over his street clothes. He added an emergency power pack, a field communicator, emergency rations, a recycler unit.

Vallant stepped from the door—and was face to face with a heavily-built Niss holding a gun like the one Vallant had first seen at the hip of the alien who had smashed his Tri-D set.

"Would you mind pointing that thing in some other direction?" Vallant started to edge past the alien. It hissed, jabbed the strange gun at him.

Vallant took a deep breath, wondering how fast

Niss reflexes were. "Perhaps I'd better explain . . . ,"
he started.

There was a sharp clatter behind the alien; the
narrow head jerked around; Vallant took a step,
hit the creature on the side of the head; it bounced
backwards, went down hard on its back; the gun
skidded away. Vallant jumped to the Niss, caught
it by the harness, dragged it into the shadow of the
shed. Jimper stepped into view.

"Well smote, Vallant!" he chirped.

"Your timing was perfect, partner!" Vallant
looked toward the lighted ship. The ground crew
was still at work, the guards lounging nearby.

"Here we go; make a wide swing. Wait until
they're all admiring me, and then run for it." Vallant started across the open ramp with a long stride.
A man with a clip-board strolled forward to meet
him. Vallant flapped the Clearance Order at him.

"All set to lift?" he barked.

"Eh? Why, no; I haven't even run idling
checks—" the man backed, keeping pace.

"Skip 'em; I'm in a hurry." Vallant brushed past,
reached the access ladder, thumbed the lock control; it cycled open. A small figure bounded from
shadow, leaped up, disappeared inside.

"Hey—"

"Clear the area; I'm lifting!" Vallant went up,
swung through the open port, clanged it behind
him, climbed up into the dim-lit control compartment, slid into the deep-padded acceleration couch,
threw the shock frame in place.

"Get on the bunk, Jimper," he called. "Lie flat
and hang on." He slammed switches. Pumps sprang
into action; a whining built, merged with the rumble
of preheat burners. The communicator light blinked
garish red on the panel.

"You in the yacht," a harsh voice blared. "Furd, or whatever your name is—"

A Niagara of sound cut off the voice. The pressure of full emergency power crushed Vallant back in the seat. On the screen, the pattern of lights that was the port dwindled, became a smudge, then glided from view as the ship angled east, driving for Deep Space.

"We're clear, Jimper," Vallant called. "Now all we have to do is figure out where we're going . . ."

6

Mars was a huge, glaring disk of mottled pink, crumbling at the edge into blackness. It lit Jimper's face eerily as he perched on the edge of the chart table, watching the planet swing ponderously past on the screen.

"Not this world, Vallant!" Jimper piped again. "Jason came with me from the world of the Blue Ice—"

"You said your country was warm and green, Jimper; with a big orange sun. Let's be realistic: Pluto is only a few degrees above absolute zero. Wherever this Galliale is, it couldn't be out there."

"You must believe Jimper, Vallant." The little creature looked appealingly across at the man. "We must go to Pluto!"

"Jimper, we need supplies, information. We'll land at Aresport, rest up, take in some of the scenery I've heard about, then see what we can find out about the old man's itinerary—"

"The Not-men will capture us!"

"Jimper, we couldn't be that important. Mars is-an autonomous planet. I know commerce has been shut off for years, but the Syndarch couldn't have any influence out here—"

"Vallant—the Not-men own all the worlds! There are no Giants but those who serve them—but for those on Earth—and why they let them live, I cannot say . . ."

"You've got a lot of wild ideas, Jimper—"

"Look!" Jimper's finger pointed at the screen. A black point was visible, drifting across the center of the planetary disc. Vallant adjusted a control, locked a tracking beam on the vessel.

"If he holds that course, we're going to scrape paint!" He keyed the communicator. *"Ariane* to Mars Tower West; I'm in my final approach pattern; request you clear the Sunday drivers out of the way."

"Pintail Red to Pintail One," a faint voice came from the speaker. "I think I've picked up our bogie; homing in on 23—268—6, sixteen kiloknots . . ."

"Pintail Red, get off the clear channel, you damned fool—" The angry voice dissolved into a blur of scrambled transmission.

"Panam Patrol—out here?" Vallant twiddled controls, frowning at the instruments. "What was that course? 23—268—6 . . ." He flipped a switch, read off the numerals which glowed on the ground glass.

"Hey, Jimper—that's us they're talking about!"

A speck separated itself from the vessel on the screen, raced toward *Ariane.*

"Hang on to your hat, Jimper," Vallant called. "He means business . . ." He slammed the drive control lever full over; the ship leaped forward.

"I guess the Ares Pavilion's out, Jimper," he said between clenched teeth, "but maybe we can find a cosy little family-type hotel on Ganymede."

7

Vallant sagged over the control panel, his un-shaven face hollow from the last week on short rations.

"*Ariane* to Ganymede Control," he croaked for the hundredth time. Ganymede Control, come in . . ."

"None will answer, Vallant," Jimper piped.

"Looks like nobody home, buddy," Vallant slumped back in the couch. "I don't understand it . . ."

"Will we go to Pluto now, Vallant?"

"You don't give up easily, do you, partner?"

Jimper sprang across, stood before Vallant, his feet planted on dial faces. "Vallant, my Land of Galliale lies beyond the snows, deep among the Blue Ice mountains. You must believe Jimper!"

"We're low on rations and my fuel banks were never intended for this kind of high-G running, weeks on end. We'll have to turn back."

"Turn back to what, Vallant? The Not-men will surely slay you—and what will happen to Jimper?"

"'There's nothing out there, Jimper!" Vallant waved a hand at the screen that reflected the black-ness of space, and the cold glitter of the distant stars. "Nothing but some big balls of ice called Ura-nus and Neptune, and the sun's just a bright star."

"There is Pluto."

"So there is . . ." Vallant raised his head, looked into the small, anxious face. "Where could this nice warm place of yours be, Jimper? Underground?"

"The sky of Galliale is wide and blue, Vallant, and graced with a golden sun."

"If I headed out that way—and failed to find Galliale—that would be the end. You know that, don't you?"

"I know, Vallant. I will not lead you awrong."

"The old man said something about mountains of ice; maybe ..." Vallant straightened. "Well, there's nothing to go back to. I've always had a yen to see what's out there. Let's go take a look, Jimper. Maybe there are still a few undreamed of things in Heaven and Earth—or beyond them."

8

The planet hung like a dull steel ball against the black; a brilliant highlight threw back the glinting reflection of the tiny disc that was the distant sun.

"All right, Jimper, guide me in," Vallant said hoarsely. "It all looks the same to me."

"When we are close, then I will know," Jimper's pointed nose seemed to quiver with eagerness as he stared into the screen. "Soon you will see, Vallant. Fair is my land of Galliale."

"I must be crazy to use my last few ounces of reaction mass to land on that," Vallant croaked. "But it's too late now to change my mind."

For the next hours, Vallant nursed the ship along, dropping closer to the icy world. Now plains of shattered ice slabs stretched endlessly below, rising at intervals into jagged peaks gleaming metallically in light as eerie as an eclipse.

"There!" Jimper piped, pointing. "The Mountains of Blue Ice ... !" Vallant saw the peaks then, rising deep blue in a sawtooth silhouette against the unending snow.

The proximity alarm clattered. Vallant pushed himself upright, read dials, adjusted the rear screen magnification. The squarish lines of a strange vessel appeared, dancing in the center of the field. Beyond, a second ship was a tiny point of reflected light.

"We're out of luck, partner," Vallant said flatly. "They must want us pretty badly."

"Make for the mountains, Vallant!" Jimper shrilled. "We can yet escape the Not-men!"

Vallant pulled himself together, hunched over the controls. "OK, Jimper, I won't give up if you won't; but that's an almighty big rabbit you're going to have to pull out of that miniature hat!"

9

It was not a good landing. Vallant unstrapped himself, got to his feet, holding onto the couch for support. Jimper crept out from under the folded blankets that had fallen on him, straightening his cap.

"We're a couple of miles short of the mark, Jimper," Vallant said. "I'm sorry; it was the best I could do."

"Now must we hasten, Vallant; deep among the blue peaks lies Galliale; long must we climb." Jimper opened his knapsack, took out a tiny miniature of a standard vacuum suit, began pulling it on. Vallant managed a laugh.

"You came prepared, fella. I guess your friend Jason made that for you."

"Even in this suit, Jimper will be cold," the long

nose seemed redder than ever. He fitted the grape-fruit-sized bowl in place over his head. Vallant checked the panel. The screens were dead; the proximity indicator dial was smashed. He donned his suit hurriedly.

"They saw us crash; they'll pick a flatter spot a few miles back; that gives us a small head start." He cycled the port open; loose objects fluttered as the air whooshed from the ship; frost formed instantly on horizontal surfaces.

Standing in the open lock, Vallant looked out at a wilderness of tilted ice slabs, fantastic architectural shapes of frost, airy bridges, tunnels, chasms of blue ice.

"Jimper—are you sure—out there . . . ?"

"High among the ice peaks," Jimper's tiny voice squeaked in Vallant's helmet. "Jimper will lead you."

"Lead on, then." Vallant jumped down into the feathery drift snow. "I'll try to follow."

The slopes were near-vertical now, polished surfaces that slanted upward, glinting darkly. The tiny arc-white sun glared between two heights that loomed overhead like cliffs. In the narrow valley between them, Vallant toiled upward, Jimper scampering ahead.

Far above a mighty river poured over a high cliff, thundering down into mist: its roar was a steady rumble underfoot.

Abruptly, Jimper's voice sounded in a shrill shout. "Vallant! Success! The Gateway lies ahead!"

Vallant struggled on another step, another, too exhausted to answer. There was a sudden heavy tremor underfoot. Jimper sprang aside. Vallant looked up; far above, a vast fragment detached itself from the wall, seeming to float downward with dream-like grace, surrounded by a convoy of lesser rubble. Great chunks smashed against the cliffsides, cascaded downward; the main mass of the avalanche shattered, dissolved into a cloud of ice-crystals. At the last moment, Jimper's warning shrilling in his ears, Vallant jumped for the shelter of a crevice. A torrent of snow poured down through the sluice-like narrow, quickly rising above the level of Vallant's hiding place. His helmet rang like a bell bombarded with gravel, then damped out as the snow packed around him. Profound silence closed in.

"Vallant!" Jimper's voice came. "Are you safe?"

"I don't know . . ." Vallant struggled, moved his arms an inch. "I'm buried; no telling how deep." He scraped at the packed snow, managed to twist himself over on his face. He worked carefully then, breaking pieces away from above, thrusting them behind. He was growing rapidly weaker; his arms seemed leaden. He rested, dug, rested . . .

The harsh white star that was the sun still hung between the ice cliffs when Vallant's groping fingers broke through and he pulled himself out to lie gasping on the surface.

"Vallant—move not or you are surely lost!" Jimper piped in his ears.

He lay, sprawled, too tired even to lift his head.

"The Not-men," Jimper went on. "Oh, they are close, Vallant."

"How close?" Vallant groaned.

"Close . . . close."

"Have they seen me?"

"Not yet, I think—but if you stir—"

"I can't stay here . . ." With an effort, Vallant got to his hands and knees, then rose, tottered on, slipping and falling. Above, Jimper danced on a ledge, frantic with apprehension.

"It lies just ahead!" He shrilled. "The Gateway to my Land of Galliale; only a little more, Vallant! A few scant paces . . ."

Ice chips flew from before Vallant's face. For a moment he stared, not understanding . . .

"They have seen you, Vallant!" Jimper screamed. "They shoot; oh, for a quiver of bolts!"

Vallant turned. A hundred yards below, a party of four suited figures—men or Niss—tramped upward. One raised the gun as a warning.

"Vallant—it is not far! Hasten!"

"It's no use," Vallant gasped. "You go ahead, Jimper. And I hope you find home again, up there in the ice."

"Jimper will not desert you, Vallant! Come, rise and try again!"

Vallant made a choking sound that was half sob, half groan. He got to his feet, lurched forward; ice smashed, a foot away. The next shot knocked him floundering into a drift of soft snow. He found his feet, struggled upward. They were shooting to intimidate, not to kill, he told himself; they needed information—and there was no escape . . .

There was a ridge ahead; Vallant paused, gathering strength. He lunged, gained the top as a near-miss kicked a great furrow in the ice; then he was sliding down the reverse slope. A dark opening showed ahead—a patch of rock, ice-free, the mouth of a cave. He rose, ran toward it, fell, then crawled . . .

It was dark suddenly; Vallant's helmet had frosted over. He groped his way on, hearing the sharp *ping!* of expanding metal.

"This way!" Jimper's voice rang in his helmet. "We will yet win free, Vallant!"

"Can't go . . . farther . . ." Vallant gasped. He was down now, lying on his face. There was a minute tugging at his arm. Through the frost melting from his faceplate, he saw Jimper's tiny figure, pulling frantically at his sleeve. He got to his knees, stood, tottered on. A powerful wind seemed to buffet at him. Wind—in this airless place . . .

Without warning, a gigantic bubble soundlessly burst; that was the sensation that Vallant felt. For a moment he stood, his senses reeling; then he shook his head, looked down over his helmet, saw packed earth walls, shored by spindly logs. Far ahead, light gleamed faintly . . .

A terrific blow knocked him flat. He rolled, found himself on his back, staring toward four dark figures, silhouetted against the luminous entrance through which he had come a minute before.

"I will bring rescuers!" Jimper's voice shrilled in Vallant's helmet.

"Run!" Vallant choked. "Don't let . . . them get you, too . . ." Faintness overtook him.

"Do not despair, Vallant," Jimper's voice seemed faint, far away. "Jimper will return . . ."

They stood over him, three Niss, grotesque and narrowfaced in their helmets, and one human, a whiskery, small-eyed man. Their mouths worked in a conversation inaudible to Vallant. Then one Niss made a downward motion with his hand; the man stepped forward, reached—

Suddenly, a wooden peg stood against the grey-green fabric of his ship-suit, upright in the center of his chest. A second magically appeared beside it—and a third. The man toppled, clutching . . . Behind him a Niss crouched, a flick of scarlet tongue visible against the gape of the white mouth.

A shaft stood abruptly in its throat. It fell backwards. Vallant raised his head; a troop of tiny red-and green-clad figures stood, setting bolts and loosing them. A Niss leaped, struck down two—then stumbled, fell, his thin chest bristling. The last Niss turned, ran from sight.

"Vallant!" Jimper's voice piped. "We are saved!"

Vallant opened his mouth to answer and darkness closed in.

10

Vallant lay on his back, feeling the gentle breeze that moved against his skin, scenting the perfumed aroma of green, growing things. Somewhere, a bird trilled a melody. He opened his eyes, looked up at a deep blue sky in which small white clouds sailed, row on row, like fairy yachts bound for some unimaginable regatta. All around were small sounds like the peeping of new-hatched chicks. He turned his head, saw a gay pavilion of red and white striped silk supported by slim poles of polished black wood topped with silver lance-heads. Under it, around it, all across the vivid green of the lawn-like meadow, thronged tiny man-like figures, gaudily dressed; the males with caps and crossbows, or armed with foot-long swords, their mates in gossamer and the sparkle of tiny gems.

At the center of the gathering, in a chair like a doll's, a corpulent elf lolled in the shadow of the pavilion. He jumped as he saw Vallant's eye upon him. He pointed, peeping excitedly in a strange, rapid tongue. A splendidly dressed warrior walked boldly toward Vallant, planted himself by his outflung hand, recited a speech.

"Sorry, Robin Goodfellow," Vallant said weakly. "I don't understand. Where's Jimper?"

The little creature before him looked about,

shouted. A bedraggled fellow in muddy brown came up between two armed warriors.

"Alas, Vallant," he piped. "All is not well in my land of Galliale."

"Jimper—you look a bit on the unhappy side, considering you brought off your miracle right on schedule."

"Something's awry, Vallant. There sits my king, Tweeple the Eater of One Hundred Tarts—and he knows not his Ambassador, Jimper!"

"Doesn't know you . . . ?" Vallant repeated.

"Jason warned me it would be so," Jimper wailed. "Yet I scarce believed him. None here knows faithful Jimper . . ."

"Are you sure you found the right town? Maybe since you left—"

"Does Jimper not know the place where he was born, where he lived while forty Great Suns came and went?" The mannikin took out a three-inch square of yellow cloth, mopped his forehead. "No, Vallant; this is my land—but it lies in the grip of strange enchantments. True, at my call the King sent warriors who guard the cave to kill the Notmen—the Evil Giants—but they would have killed you, too, Vallant, had I not pleaded your helpless state, and swore you came as a friend. We Spril-folk have ever feared the memory of the Evil Giants."

"Kill me?" Vallant started to laugh, then remembered the shafts bristling in the bodies of the Niss. "I've come too far to get myself killed now."

"Near you were to a longer journey still, Vallant. I know not how long the king will stay his hand."

"Where are we, Jimper? How did we get here?"

"The king's men dragged you here on a mat of reeds."

"But—how did we get out of the cave?"

"Through the Portal, Vallant—as I said, yet you would not believe!"

"I'm converted," Vallant said. "I'm here—wherever *here* is. But I seem to remember a job of world-saving I was supposed to do."

Jimper looked stricken. "Alas, Vallant! King Tweeple knows naught of these great matters! It was he whom Jason told of the Great Affairs beyond the Portal, and the part the Folk must play."

"So I'm out of a job?" Vallant lay for a moment, feeling the throb in his head, the ache that spread all through his shoulder and back.

"Maybe I'm dreaming," he said aloud. He made a move to sit up—

"No, Vallant! Move not, on your life!" Jimper shouted. "The King's archers stand with drawn bows if you should rise to threaten them!"

Vallant turned his head; a phalanx of tiny bowmen stood, arrows aimed, a bristling wall of foot-tall killers. Far away, beyond the green meadow, the clustered walls and towers of a miniature city clung to a hillside.

"Didn't you tell the King that I came to help him?"

"I pledged my life on it, Vallant—but he names me stranger. At last he agreed that so long as you lay sorely hurt, ho harm could come of you—but take care! The King need but say the word, and you are lost, Vallant!"

"I can't lie here forever, Jimper. What if it rains?"

"They prepare a pavilion for you, Vallant—but first must we prove your friendship."

Jimper mopped his face again. Vallant stared up at the sky.

"How badly am I hurt?" Vallant moved slightly,

testing his muscles. "I don't even remember being hit."

"A near-miss, meant to warn you, Vallant—but great stone chips are buried in your flesh. The King's surgeons could remove them—if he would so instruct them. Patience now, Vallant; I will treat with him again."

Vallant nodded, watched as Jimper, flanked by his guards, marched back to stand before the pudgy ruler. More piping talk ensued. Then Jimper returned, this time with two companions in crumpled conical hats.

"These are the royal surgeons, Vallant," he called. "They will remove the flints from your back. You have the royal leave to turn over—but take care; do not alarm him with sudden movements."

Vallant complied, groaning; he felt a touch, twisted his head to see a two-foot ladder lean against his side. A small face came into view at the top, apprehensive under a pointed hat. Vallant made what he hoped was an encouraging smile.

"Good morning, doctor," he said. "I guess you feel like a sailor getting ready to skin a whale . . ." then he fainted.

11

Vallant sat on a rough log bench, staring across the four-foot stockade behind which he had been fenced for three weeks now—as closely as he could estimate time, in a land where the sun stood overhead while he slept, wakened, and slept again. Now it was behind the tops of the towering poplar-like trees, and long shadows lay across the lawns under a sky of green and violet and flame. A mile away, lights glittered from a thousand tiny windows in the toy city of Galliale.

"If I could but convince the King," Jimper piped dolefully, a woebegone expression on his pinched features. "But fearful is the heart of Tweeple; not like the warrior kings of old, who slew the Evil Giants."

"These Evil Giants—were they the Niss?"

"Well might it be, Vallant. The legends tell that they were ugly as trolls and evil beyond the imagining of man or Spril. Ah, but those were brave days, when the great Giants had fallen, and only the Folk fought on."

"Jimper, do you suppose there's any truth in these legends of yours?"

The tiny mannikin stared. "Truth? True they be as carven stone, Vallant! True as the bolt sped from my bow! Look there!" He pointed to a gaunt stone structure rising from a twilit hill beyond the forest to the east.

"Is that a dream? But look at the stones of it! Plain it is that Giants raised it once, long and long ago."

"What is it?"

"The Tower of the Forgotten; the legend tells that in it lies a treasure so precious that for it a King would give his crown; but the Thing of Fear, the Scaled One, the Dread Haik set to guard it by the Evil Giants, wards it well, pent in the walls."

"Oh, a dragon, too. I must say you have a completely equipped mythology, Jimper. What about these Great Giants—I take it they were friendly with the Spril?"

"Great were the Illimpi, Vallant, and proud were the Spril to serve them. But now they are dead, vanished all away; and yet, some say they live on, in their distant place, closed away from their faithful Folk by spells of magic, and the Scaled Haik of the Niss."

"Jimper—you don't believe in magic?"

"Do I not? Have I not seen the Cave of No Return with my own eyes—and worse, passed through it?"

"That's the tunnel we came in by, Jimper. You went through it with your friend Jason on the way out—and now you've returned."

"Ah, have I indeed, Vallant? True it is I passed through the Cave—and only my sworn fealty to my King forced me to it—but have I returned in truth? Who is there who welcomes my return?"

"I admit that's a puzzler . . ."

"Tales have I heard of others, long ago, who came from the cave, strangers to the Tribe of Spril—and yet of our blood and customs. Always they talked of events unknown, and swore they had but ventured out into the Blue Ice—and now I am of their number; the stranger in his own land, whom no one knows."

Vallant rose, looking across toward the city. A long procession of torch-bearers was filing from the city gates, winding across the dark plain toward Vallant's stockade. "It looks as though we have visitors coming, Jimper."

"Woe, Vallant! This means the King has decided your fate! Well has he wined this night—and drink was never known to temper the mercy of the King!"

"If they're coming here to fill me full of arrows, I'm leaving!"

"Wait, Vallant! The captain of the guard is a decent fellow; I'll go to meet them. If they mean you ill, I'll . . . I'll snatch a torch and wave it thus . . ." he made circular motions above his head.

Vallant nodded. "OK, partner—but don't get yourself in trouble."

Half an hour later, the cavalcade halted before Vallant, Jimper striding beside the breast-plated Captain. He ran forward.

"Mixed news, Vallant; This is the judgement of the King: that you shall stand before him in his Hall, and show proof that you are friend to the Spril-folk; and if you fail . . ."

"If I fail?" Vallant prompted.

"Then shall you enter the Cave of No Return, whence no man or Spril has ever come back."

The main avenue of the city of Galliale was ten feet wide, cobbled with cut stones no bigger than dice, winding steeply up between close-crowded houses, some half-timbered, others of gaily patterned masonry, with tiny shops below, gay with lights and merchandise, and open casement windows above, from which small, sharp-nosed faces thrust, staring at the looming giant who strode along, surrounded by the helmeted warriors of the King, toward the dazzling tower of light that was the Royal Palace of Tweeple the Eater of One hundred Tarts.

"I don't understand why his highness isn't content to let me sit out there under my canopy and smell the flowers," Vallant said to Jimper, who rode on his shoulder. "I've even volunteered to be his royal bodyguard—"

"He sees you grow well and strong, Vallant. He fears you may yet turn on the Folk as did the Evil Giants in the olden time."

"Can't you convince him I'm the good variety? I'd be handy to have around if that Niss who escaped came back with a couple of his friends."

"Never will he return, Vallant!" All who enter the Cave—"

"I know—but if he sends *me* out there in the cold, I'm likely to turn around and sneak right back in—tradition or no."

"Ah, if Jason were but here to vouch for you," Jimper piped. "Well he knew the tongue of the Spril, and wondrous the tales he told; charmed was King Tweeple, and many were the honors of Jason the Giant. But now, alas, the King knows naught of all these things."

"'How did Jason happen to find Galliale?"

"He told of a great battle fought between the worlds, where Niss died like moths in the flame under the mighty weapons of the men of Earth—"

"The old man talked to me about a war; he said we lost."

"Jason's ship was hurt," Jimper went on. "He fell far, far, but at last brought the ship to ground among the Blue Ice crags. He saw the Portal among the snows—the same in which we fought the Notmen, Vallant—and so he came to Fair Galliale."

"And then he left again—"

"But not until he had tarried long and long among us, Vallant. At his wish, sentinels were posted, day and night, to watch through the Cave of No Return, which gives a fair view of the icy slopes and the plain beyond, for sight of men. Often, when he had drunk a hogshead or two of the King's best ale, he would groan, and cry aloud to know how it went with the battle of the Giants; but he knew the magic of the Cave, and so he waited. And then one day, when he had grown old and bent, the sentries gave him tidings that a strange vessel lay in view beyond the Cave. Grieved was the King, and he swore that he would set his bowmen to guard the entrance to that enchanted path, that Jason the

Teller of Tales might not walk down it to be seen
no more; but Jason only smiled and said that go
he would, asking only that an Ambassador be sent
with him, to treat with the Giants; and it was I,
Jimper, warrior and scholar, whom the King
chose."

That was quite an honor; too bad he doesn't remember it; and I'm sorry I don't know any stories
I could charm the old boy with. I haven't made
much headway with the language yet."

"Long before Jason there was another Giant who
came to Galliale," Jimper chirped. "No talker was
he, but a mighty Giant of valor. The tale tells how
he went in against the Scaled One to prove his love
to the King of those times. I heard the tale from
my grandfather's father, when I was but a fingerling,
when we sat in ring under the moons and talked
of olden times. He came from the Cave—hurt, as
you were, Vallant. And the King of those times
would have slain him—but in sign of friendship,
he entered the Tower of the Forgotten, there to
battle the Fanged One who guards the treasures.
Then did the king know that he was friend indeed,
and of the race of goodly Giants—"

"And what happened to him in the end?"

"Alas, never did he return from the Tower, Vallant—but honored was his memory!"

"That's a cheery anecdote. Well, we'll find out
in a minute what Tweeple has in mind."

The procession had halted in the twenty-foot
Grand Plaza before the palace gates. The warriors
formed up in two ranks, flanking Vallant, bows
ready. Beyond a foot-high spike-topped wall, past
a courtyard of polished stones as big as dominoes,
the great two-foot high entrance to the palace
blazed with light. Beyond it, Vallant caught a

glimpse of intricately carved paneling, tiny-patterned tapestries, and a group of Spril courtiers in splendid costumes, bowing and curtsying as the plump elf-king waddled forth to stand, hands on hips, staring up at Vallant.

He spoke in a shrill voice, waving ringed hands, pausing now and again to quaff a thimble-sized goblet offered by a tiny Spril no taller than a chipmunk.

He finished, and a servant handed him a scarlet towel to dry his pink face. Jimper, who had climbed down and taken up a position in the row of Spril beside the King, came across to Vallant.

"The King says . . ." He paused, swallowed. "That his royal will is . . ."

"Go ahead," Vallant urged, eyeing the ranks of ready bowmen. "Tell me the worst."

"To prove your friendship, Vallant—you must enter the Tower of the Forgotten, and there slay the Fanged One, the Scaled One, the Eater of Fire!"

Vallant let out a long sigh. "You had me worried there for a minute, Jimper," he said, almost gaily. "I thought I was going to provide a target for the royal artillery—"

"Jest not, Vallant!" Jimper stamped angrily. "Worse by far is the fate decreed by the King! Minded am I to tell him so—"

"Don't get yourself in hot water, Jimper; it's OK. I'm satisfied with the assignment."

"But, Vallant! No one—not even a Great Giant —can stand against the Fearsome One whom the Evil Giants set to guard the tower!"

"Will he be satisfied if I go into the Tower and come out again alive—even if I don't find the dragon?"

"Delude yourself no more, Vallant! The Scaled One waits there—"

"Still—"

"Yes, to enter the Tower is enough. But—"

"Fair enough. I may not come out dragging the body by the tail, but the legend won't survive the experience. When do I go?"

"As soon as may be . . ." Jimper shuddered, then drew himself erect. "But have no fear, Vallant; Jimper will be at your side."

Vallant smiled down at the tiny warrior. "That's a mighty brave thing to do, Jimper; I wish I could put your mind at rest about the dragon."

Jimper looked up at him, hands on hips. "And I, Vallant, wish that I could stir in you some healthful fear." He turned, strode back across the courtyard to the King, saluted, spoke briefly. A murmur ran out from the group of courtiers; then a treble cheer went up, while tiny caps whirled high. The King signaled, and white-clad servitors surged forward, setting up tables, laying out heaped platters, rolling great one-quart barrels into position.

"The King decrees a night of feasting, Vallant!" Jimper chirped, running to him. "And you too shall dine!"

Vallant watched while a platform normally used for speeches was set up and vivid rugs as fine as silk laid out on it; then he seated himself and accepted a barrel of ale, raised it in a toast to the King.

"Eat, drink, and be merry . . ." he called.

"If you can," Jimper said, mournful again, "knowing what tomorrow will bring."

12

In the fresh light of morning, Vallant strode across the emerald velveteen of the Plain of Galli-ale, feeling the cool air in his face, ignoring the throb in his head occasioned by last night's five bar-rels of royal ale, watching the silhouette of the tower ahead growing larger against the dawn sky. A long sword—a man-sized duplicate of the tiny one at Jimper's belt—brought from the King's trea-sury of Ancient Things for his use, swung at his side; in his hand he carried a nine-foot spear with a head of polished brass. Behind him trotted a full battalion of the Royal guard, lances at the ready.

"I'll have to admit that King Tweeple went all-out in support of the expedition, Jimper," Vallant said. "Even if he did claim he'd never heard of your friendly giant."

"Strange are the days when valued tales of old are unknown to the king. But no matter—pleased is he to find a champion."

"Well, I hope he's just as pleased when I come out and report that the Scaled One wasn't there after all."

Jimper looked up from where he scampered at Vallant's side. He was splendid now in a new scarlet cloak and a pink cap with a black plume. "Vallant, the Scaled One dwells in the Tower, as sure as blos-soms bloom and kings die!"

Another quarter hour's walk brought Vallant and his escort through the forest of great conifers and out onto a wild-grown slope where long mounds overgrown with vines and brambles surrounded the monolithic tower on its crest. Near at hand, a slab of white stone gleamed through underbrush. Vallant went close, pulled the growth away to reveal a weathered bench-top.

"Hey, it looks as though someone used to live here—and a giant at that." He glanced at the tumuli, some large, some small, forming an intersecting geometric pattern that reached up to the tower's base.

"Those are the ruins of buildings, and walls; this whole hilltop was built up at one time—a long time ago."

"Once those Giants whom the Spril served dwelt here," Jimper piped. "Then the Evil Giants came and slew our masters with weapons of fire. There was a great king among the Spril in those days, Vallant: Josro the Sealer of Gates. He it was who led the Folk in the war against the Ugly Ones." He looked up at the Tower. "But, alas, the Scaled One lives on to wall away the treasure of the Illimpi."

"Well, let's see if we can go finish the job, Jimper." Vallant went up past the mounded ruins. At the top he paused, looking back down the silent slope. "It must have been beautiful once, Jimper," he said. "A palace of white marble, and the view all across the valley . . ."

"Fair it was, and enchanted is its memory," Jimper said. "Long have we feared this place, but now we come to face its dreads. Lead on, Vallant; Jimper is at your side!"

A shrill trumpet note pierced the air. The troop of the King's Lancers had halted. Their captain called an order; the two-foot lances swung down in a salute.

"They wait here," Jimper said. "The King will not risk them closer—and they guard our retreat, if the Scaled One should break out, which Fate forfend!"

Vallant returned the salute with a wave of his hand. "I guess if you believe in dragons, to come this far is pretty daring." He glanced down at Jimper. "That makes you a regular hero, partner."

"And what of you, Vallant! In your vast shadow Jimper walks boldly, but you go with only your lance and blade to meet the Terrible One!"

"That doesn't count; I don't really expect to meet him."

Now four warriors came forward, stumbling under the weight of a foot-long box slung from their shoulders by leather straps. They lowered it gingerly before Vallant, scampered back to the ranks.

"What's this, a medal—already?" Vallant pressed a stud on the side of the flat box; its lid popped up. Nestled in a fitted case lay a heavy electro-key of unfamiliar design. Vallant picked it up, whistled in surprise.

"Where did this come from, Jimper?"

"When long ago the Spril-Folk slew the Evil Ones, this did they find among the spoils. Long have we guarded it, until our Goodly Giants should come again."

Vallant examined the heavy key. "This is a beautiful job of microtronic engineering, Jimper. I'm beginning to wonder who these Giants of yours were." He went up the last few yards of the vine-grown slope to the vast door of smooth, dark material which loomed up in the side of the tower; the structure itself, Vallant saw, was not of stone, but of a weathered synthetic, porous and discolored with age.

"I'd give a lot to know who built this, Jimper," he said. "It must have been a highly technical people; that stuff looks like it's been there for a lot of years."

"Great were our Giants, and great was their fall. Long have we waited their return. Now it may be that you, Vallant, and Jason, are the first of those ancient ones to come back to your Galliale."

" 'Fraid not, Jimper. But we can still be friends." Vallant studied the edge of the door.

"Looks like we'll have to dig, Jimper. The dirt's packed in here, no telling how deep."

Jimper unsheathed his eight-inch sword, handed it to Vallant. "Use this; a nobler task could not be found for it."

Vallant set to work. Behind him, the ranks of the bowmen stood firm, watching. The unyielding surface of the door extended down six inches, a foot, two feet, before he came to its lower edge.

"We've got a job ahead, partner," he said. "I hope this snoozing dragon of yours is worth all the effort."

"For my part," Jimper said, "I hope the sound of our digging awakens him not too soon."

Two hours later, with the door cleared of the packed soil and an arc excavated to accommodate its swing, Vallant returned Jimper's sword, then took the key from the box.

"Let's hope it still works; I'd hate to try to batter my way past that . . ." He lifted the key to the slot in the door; there was a deep-seated *click!*, a rumble of old gears.

"It looks as though we're in business."

Vallant hammered back the heavy locking bar that secured the massive door; then, levering with his swordblade, he swung the thick panel back, looked into a wide corridor inches deep in dust. The Captain of the Guard and four archers came up, waiting nervously to close the door as soon as Vallant was safely inside. Jimper sneezed. Vallant stooped, lifted him to his shoulder. He waved to the escort, who raised a nervous cheer. Then he stepped into the dust of the corridor, watched as the door slowly clanked shut behind him.

"We're in, Jimper," he said. "Now—which way to the dragon?"

Jimper fingered his crossbow, staring ahead along the dim hall. "H-he could be anywhere . . ."

"Let's take a look around." Vallant explored the length of the corridor which circled the tower against the outer wall, floundering through dust drifted deep under the loopholes high in the walls. At one point a great heap almost blocked the passage. He kicked at it, yelped; rusted metal plates showed where the covering of dust was disturbed.

"It looks like a dump for old armor," he complained, clambering over the six-foot high obstruction. "Maybe this was an early junkyard . . ."

Jimper muttered fretfully, "Walk softly, Vallant . . ."

They completed the circuit, then took a stairway, mounted to a similar passage at a higher level. Everywhere the mantle of dust lay undisturbed. They found rooms, empty except for small metal objects of unfamiliar shape, half buried in dust. Once Vallant stooped, picked up a statuette of bright yellow metal.

"Look at this, Jimper," he said. "It's a human figure!"

"True," Jimper agreed, squinting at the three-inch image. "No Spril form is that."

"This place must have been built by men, Jimper! Or by something so like them that the differences don't show. And yet, we've only had space travel for a couple of centuries—"

"Long have the Giants roamed the worlds, Vallant."

"Maybe—but humans have been Earth-bound until just lately. It's comforting to know that there are other creatures somewhere that look something like us—I guess."

They followed corridors, mounted stairs, prowled through chambers large and small. Faint light from tiny apertures in the walls was the only illumination. High in the tower, they came to a final narrow flight of steps. Vallant looked up.

"Well, if he's not up here, I think we can consider the mission accomplished."

"Certain it is that somewhere lurks the Dread One," Jimper chirped. "Now l-let him b-beware!"

"That's the spirit." Vallant went up the stairs—gripping his sword now in spite of his scepticism; if there were anything alive in the tower, it would have to be here . . .

He emerged in a wide, circular room, high-vaulted, thick with dust. A lustrous cube, white, frosty-surfaced, twelve feet on a side, was mounted two feet clear of the floor at the exact center of the chamber. It seemed almost to glow in the dim room. Cautiously, Vallant circled it. The four sides were identical, unadorned, shimmering white.

Vallant let his breath out, sheathed the sword. "That's that," he said. "No dragon."

Perched on his shoulder, Jimper clutched his neck.

"I fear this place, Vallant," he piped. "We have blundered—I know not how . . ."

"We're all right, old timer," Vallant soothed. "Let's take a look around. Maybe we can pick up a souvenir to take back to old Tweeple—"

"Vallant, speak not with disrespect of my King!" Jimper commanded.

"Sorry." Vallant's boots went in to the ankle as he crossed the drifted floor to the glistening polyhedron; he touched its surface; it was cool, slippery as graphite.

"Funny stuff," he said. "I wonder what it's for?"

"Vallant, let us not linger here."

Vallant turned, looked around the gloomy room. Vague shapes bulked under the dust blanket. He went to a tablelike structure, blew at it, raising a cloud that made Jimper sneeze. He brushed at the array of dials and bright-colored knobs and buttons that emerged from the silt.

"It's some kind of control console, Jimper! What do you suppose it controls?"

"L-let us depart, Vallant!" Jimper squeaked. "I like not these ancient rooms!"

"I'll bet it has something to do with that . . ." Vallant nodded toward the cube. "Maybe if I push a couple of buttons . . ." He jabbed a finger at a large scarlet lever in the center of the panel. It clicked down decisively.

"Vallant—meddle not with these mysteries!" Jimper screeched. He crouched on Vallant's shoulder, eyes fixed on the lever.

"Nothing happened," Vallant said. "I guess it was too much to expect . . ." He paused. A draft stirred in the room; dust shifted, moving on the tabletop.

"Hey—" Vallant started.

Jimper huddled against his neck, moaning. Dust was flowing across the floor, drifting toward the glossy surface of the cube, whipping against it—and beyond. Vallant felt the draft increase, fluttering the fabric of his shipsuit. The dust was rising up in a blinding cloud now; Vallant ducked his head, started toward the door. The wind rose to whirlwind proportions, hurling him against the wall; air was whining in through the loopholes; dust whipped and streamed, flowing to the face of the cube, which glared through the obscuring veil now with a cold white light. Vallant lunged again for the door, met a blast like a sand-storm that sent him reeling, Jimper still clinging to his perch. He struggled to a sheltered angle between floor and wall, watched as the wind whirled the dust away, scouring the floor clean, exposing a litter of metallic objects. Nearby lay a finger-ring, an ornate badge, an odd-shaped object that might have been a hand-gun. Beyond were a scatter of polished metal bits, the size and shape of shark teeth.

Now, suddenly, the wind was lessening. The white-glaring rectangle was like an open window with a view of a noon-day fog. The last swirls of dust flashed toward it and were gone. The shrilling of the gale died. The room was still again.

"Now must we flee . . ." Jimper whistled; he flapped his cloak, settled his pink cap, edging toward the door. Vallant got to his feet, spitting dust. "Not yet, Jimper. Let's take a look at this . . ." He went close to the glowing square, stared at it, reached out a hand . . .

And encountered nothing.

He jerked the hand back quickly.

"Whew! That's cold!" He massaged the numbed hand. "Half a second, and it was stiff!"

Somewhere, far away, a faint, metallic clanking sounded.

"Vallant! He comes!" Jimper screeched.

"Calm down, Jimper! We're all right. It was a little thick there for a minute, but I suppose that was just some sort of equalization process. Or maybe this thing is a central cleaning device; sort of a building-sized vacuum cleaner . . ."

Abruptly, the panel before Vallant dimmed. Shapes whipped across it. The shadowy outlines of a room appeared, sharpened into vivid focus. Sounds came through: an electronic hum, the insistent pinging of a bell, then a clump of hurried feet.

A man appeared, stood staring across at Vallant, as through an open doorway.

Or almost a man.

He was tall—near seven feet, and broad through the shoulders. His hair curled close to his head, glossy black as Persian lamb, and through it, the points of two short, blunt horns protruded, not quite symmetrically, on either side of the nobly rounded skull.

He spoke—staccato words in a language strange to Vallant. His voice was deep, resonant.

"Sorry, sir," Vallant got out, staring. "I'm afraid I don't understand . . ."

The horned man leaned closer. His large, dark-blue eyes were fixed on Vallant's.

"Lla," he said commandingly.

Vallant shook his head. He tried a smile; the majestic figure before him was not one which inspired the lighter emotions. "I guess—" he started, then paused to clear his throat. "I guess we've stumbled onto something a little bigger than I expected . . ."

The horned man made an impatient gesture as Vallant paused. He repeated the word he had spoken. Vallant felt a tug at the knee of his suit.

"Vallant!" Jimper peeped. Vallant looked down. "Not now, Jimper—"

"I think—I think Jimper understands what the Great Giant means. In the ceremony of the crowning of the king, there is a phrase, "*'qa ic' lla* . . .' It is spoken in the old tongue, the speech of long ago; and the wise elders say those words mean *'when he speaks'!* He would have you talk . . ."

The horned giant leaned toward Vallant, as though to see below the edge of the invisible plane between them. Vallant stooped, raised Jimper up chest-high. The mannikin straightened himself; then, standing on Vallant's hand, he doffed his feathered cap, bent nearly double in a deep bow.

"*Ta p'ic ih sya, Illimpi,*" he chirped.

A remarkable change came over the horned man's face. His eyes widened; his mouth opened— then a vast smile lit his face like a floodlight.

"*I' Ipliti!*" he roared. He turned, did something out of sight of Vallant beyond the edge of the cube, whirled back. He spoke rapidly to Jimper. The little creature spread his hands, looking contrite.

"*N'iqi,*" he said. "*N'iqi, Illimi.*"

The giant nodded quickly, looked keenly at Vallant.

"*Lla, Vallant,*" he commanded.

He knows my name . . ." Vallant gulped. "What am I supposed to talk about?"

"He is a Great Giant," Jimper peeped excitedly. "Well he knows Jimper's kind, from of old. Tell him all, Vallant—all that has befallen the race of Giants since last the Portal closed."

13

Vallant talked for five minutes, while the giant beyond the invisible barrier adjusted controls out of sight below the Portal's edge.

". . . when I came to, I was here—"

The giant nodded suddenly. "Well enough," he said clearly. Vallant stared in surprise. The horned man's lips, he noticed, did not move in synchronization with his words.

"Now," the giant said, "what world are you?"

"What . . . how . . . ?" Vallant started.

"A translating device; I am Cessus the Communicator. What world are you?"

"Well, I would have said I was on Pluto, except that . . . I couldn't be. And on the other hand, I must be . . ."

"Your language . . . A strange tongue it is; none that I have known in my days in the Nex. Best I find you on the Locator . . ." He flipped unseen levers; his eyes widened.

"Can it be?" He stared at Vallant. "A light glows on my panel that has not been lit these ten Grand Eons . . . that of Lost Galliale . . ."

Vallant nodded eagerly. "That's right—Galliale is what Jimper calls the place. But—"

"And your people; are all—as you?"

"More or less."

"None have these?" he pointed.

"Horns? No. And this isn't my home world, of course. I come from Terra—third from the sun."

"But—what of the Illimpi of Galliale?" The giant's face was taut with strain.

"Nobody lives here but Jimper's people. Right, Jimper?"

"True," Jimper spoke up. "Once the Evil Giants —foes of the Great Giants—came; but from thicket and burrow we crept, after the last Great Giant fell. We loosed our bolts to find their marks in vile green hide, then slipped away to fight again. So we dealt with them all, we bowmen, for against our secret bolts, of what avail their clumsy lightnings? The last of them fled away down the Cave of No Return, and free at last was my land of Galliale from their loathsome kind. Now long have we waited for our

Giants to come back; and in their absence have we tilled and spun and kept fair the land."

"Well done, small warrior," Cessus said. He studied Vallant's face. "You are akin to us—that much is plain to see; and you dwell on the double world that lies third from the sun—so some few survivors made good their secret flight there—"

"Survivors of what?"

"Of the onslaught of those you call the Niss."

"Then—what the old man said was true? They're invaders—"

"That, and more, Vallant! They are the bringers of darkness, the all-evil, the wasters of worlds!"

"But—they haven't wasted the Earth; you hardly notice them; they're just a sort of police force—"

"They are a poison that stains the Galaxy. Long ago, they came, destroying—but listen; this was the way of it:

"Ages past, we Illimpi built the Portal—this block of emptiness before which you stand—linking the star-clouds. We sent colonists into the fair new world of Galliale—adventurers, man and woman, the brave ones who never could return; and with them went the Spril-Folk, the faithful Little People.

"They thrived, and in time they built a Gate—a useful link to a sunny world they called Olantea, circling in the fifth orbit of a yellow sun twenty light-years distant. There they built cities, planted gardens that were a delight to the senses.

"Then, without warning, the Niss came to Galliale, pouring through the Gateway, armed with weapons of fire. Swift and terrible was their assault, and deadly the gases they spread abroad, and the crawling vermin to spread their plagues. The peaceful Illimpi of Galliale battled well, and volunteers rushed through the Great Portal to their aid. But deadly were the weapons of the Niss; they carried the Tower of the Portal and some few, mad with blood-lust, rushed through it, never to return. Then the Portal failed, and lost was our link with our colony. The long centuries have passed, and never did we know till now how it fared with lost Galliale."

"So the Spril finished off the Niss, after the Niss had killed the Illimpi? Nice work, Jimper. But how did you manage it?"

"Proof were we against their sickness," Jimper piped. "But no defense had they against our bows."

"If the Niss are such killers, why haven't they used their weapons on us? The story the Syndarch tells is that they're our great friends, sharing their wisdom—"

"Proof have we seen of that lie," Jimper chirped. "Deep are the plots of the Niss."

"It is the Portal they seek," Cessus said. "All who came to Galliale were lost to them."

"Just a minute," Vallant cut in. "I'm lost. The Niss came through the Gateway from Olantea—but that was held by the Illimpi. The Niss must have hit them, and captured the Gateway—which I take it is some sort of matter transmitter. But why wasn't Galliale warned? And why is it none of the Galliales escaped through the Portal here, back to the home world? And how did the Gateway get shifted from Olantea to Pluto?"

Cessus was frowning in puzzlement. "Do you not know, Vallant—"

"Vallant!" Jimper cocked his head. "The Scaled One—I hear him stir!"

"It's your imagination, Jimper. We've explored the whole building, and didn't find him, remember?"

The horned man was looking at Jimper. "What manner of creature is this Scaled One?"

"It's just a superstition of Jimper's—" Vallant started.

"A Haik, Great Giant," Jimper shrilled. "A guardian set by the Niss when they had closed the Portal against the Illimpi, before they fared forth against the Spril, from which adventure no Niss returned—"

Cessus whirled on Vallant. "How have you restrained the beast?"

Vallant's mouth opened. "I hope you don't mean—" he began.

There was a sudden clangor as of armor clashing against stone.

"The Fanged One comes!" Jimper shrilled.

"What weapon have you!" Cessus rapped out.

"Just this ham-slicer . . ." Vallant gripped the sword-hilt. "But I have a feeling it's not quite what the program requires . . ."

The clatter was louder now; Jimper screeched; the horned Giant whirled to reach behind the screen's edge—

There was a screech of tortured steel from the doorway; a hiss like an ancient steam-whistle split the air. Vallant spun, stared at a vast *thing*—like a jumble of rusted fragments of armor plate, wedged in the doorway, clawing with legs like gleaming black cables three inches thick, armed with mirror-bright talons which raked grooves in the hard floor as though it were clay. From a head like a fang-spiked mace, white eyes with pinpoint pupils glared in insane ferocity. The Haik surged, sending chips of the door-frame flying as it forced its bulk through the narrow way.

"Ye Gods!" Vallant yelled. "Jimper, why didn't you tell me this thing really existed!"

"Tell you I did, Vallant; now slay it with your sword!"

"What good is a hat-pin against a man-eating rhino like that!" Vallant backed, watching as the material of the wall chipped and crumbled under the force of the Haik's thrust. His eye fell on the gun-like object on the floor. He jumped for it, caught it up, raised it and pressed the button on its side. A lance of blue flame licked out, touched the Haik's snout. The monster clashed its jaws, gained another foot. The flame played on its cheek, dimmed abruptly, fell back to a weak yellowish glow, died with a harsh buzz. Vallant threw the weapon from him.

"Vallant!" Jimper shrieked. "The door-frame! It crumbles!"

"Sorry, Jimper! I guess we'll just have to round up a posse and come back after him!" Vallant grabbed up the little creature, stepped to the screen—

"No, Vallant!" the horned man shouted—

"Here I come, ready or not—" Vallant closed his eyes, and stepped through the Portal.

14

There was an instant of bitter cold; then silence, a touch of cool air, an odor of almonds . . .

Vallant opened his eyes. A great, dim, vaulted hall arched high above him; far away, mighty columns loomed into shadows. Beyond, an iodine-colored wall towered up, misty with distance, decorated in patterns of black lines set off with glittering flecks of gold and copper.

"Where is he?" Vallant blurted, staring around. "What happened to Cessus the Communicator?"

Jimper huddled against Vallant, peering up into the mists far overhead. "Lost are we now, Vallant. Nevermore will we see the spires of Galliale—nor the drab cities of your world . . ."

"He was right here—and the room behind him . . ."

"Dread are the mysteries of the Great Giants . . ." Jimper keened.

"Well," Vallant laughed shakily. "At least we left the Haik behind." He sheathed the unused sword. "I wonder who lives here." Faint echoes rolled back from the distant wall. "We're in a building of some kind; look at this floor, Jimper. Slabs the size of tennis courts. Talk about Giants . . ."

"Vallant—can we not go back? I dread the Haik less than I fear this place of echoes."

"Well . . ." Vallant studied the empty air around them. "I don't see anything that looks like a Portal. Maybe if we just feel our way . . ." He took a cautious step; Jimper wriggled down, darted ahead. He paused, puzzled, turned back—and froze, staring. Vallant whirled. At the spot where he had stood, a glossy black cable, dagger tipped, writhed in the air three feet above the stone floor.

"The Haik!" Jimper squealed. With a deafening screech, the many-spiked head of the monster appeared, followed an instant later by its two-ton bulk, crashed thunderously through the Portal. For a moment it crouched as though confused; then at a sound from Jimper, it wheeled with murderous speed on its intended victims.

Vallant whipped out the sword. "Run, Jimper. Maybe I can slow him down for a second or two—"

Jimper snatched the crossbow from his back, fitted a six-inch quarrel in place, drew and let fly; the dart whistled past Vallant's head, glanced off the Haik's armor. The creature gaped tooth-ringed jaws, dug in its talons for the spring—

There was a sudden rush of air, a shriek of wind. From nowhere, a vast grid slammed down, struck with an impact that jarred the floor, knocked Vallant from his feet. He scrambled up, saw the grid receding as rapidly as it had come. The broken thing that had been the Haik flicked cable-legs in a last convulsion, then lay, a shattered, rusted hulk, leaking thin fluid against the stone.

"Whatever that was," Vallant said shakily, "it just missed us . . ." He looked up. Far up in the dimness, a great pale shape hung, a misty oblong, with smaller dark patches, whose outline wavered and flowed, bulging and elongating . . .

Then it withdrew and was gone.

"Jimper!" Vallant croaked. "Did you see that?"

"I saw naught, Vallant," Jimper shrilled. "The Haik charged and then—I know not."

"It was . . ." Vallant paused to gulp. "A face . . . a huge, rubbery face, a mile long and five miles up . . . and I'd swear it was looking right at me!"

"Another invasion of mind-fleas in the Hall," said a voice as clear as engraved print.

"Ill-struck, Brometa," a second voice answered. *"I hear their twittering still."*

"Vallant!" Jimper gasped. "Those there are who speak close by—and in the tongue of the Spril-Folk —yet I see them not . . ."

"N-nonsense," Vallant gulped. "They're speaking English . . . But where are they?"

"We should have plugged the hole they burrowed last time," the silent voice said, *"Here, give me the whisk; I'll attend to these fleas—"*

"No!" Vallant yelled at the top of his lungs, staring upward into the formless shadows. "We're not fleas!"

"*Yapud! Did you hear words amid the twitterings just now?*"

There was a pause; distant rumblings sounded. "*You must have imagined it, Brometa—*"

"*I heard it just as you raised the whisk—*"

"Don't do it!" Vallant bellowed.

"*There! Surely you heard that! It rang in my mind like a light-storm.*"

"*Yes, I do believe you're right!*"

Staring upward, Vallant saw the vast cloud-face appear again, its shape changing.

"*I see nothing, Yapud.*"

"We're friendly!" Vallant shouted. "Don't swat us!"

"*These fleas have the same irritating way of projecting thought forms out of all proportion to their size—*"

"*More of those hate-scorched vermin who infested the Hall last Great Cycle? Swat them at once!*"

"*No, this is another breed. Those others—Niss, they called themselves—what a vicious mind-stink they raised before we fumigated! Hmmm. This one seems quite different, Yapud.*"

"*Vermin are vermin! Give me the whisk—*"

"*Hold! Little enough I have to divert me here; let me converse awhile with these noisy fleas.*"

"What transpires, Vallant?" Jimper peeped. He gazed worriedly up at Vallant. "Who speaks in Jimper's head?"

"I don't know, Jimper—but it's something that thinks I'm a flea, and doesn't even know about you."

"*Here, you fleas; I'll put a paper on the floor; step upon it, that I may lift you up where I can lay eyes on you.*"

There was a great rushing of air. A vast, white

shape rushed down, blotting out the mists above. Vallant and Jimper dropped flat, clung to crevices in the floor against the rush of air that whistled past. An immense, foot-thick platform thudded to the floor fifty feet away, stretching off into the distance. The wind howled and died.

"We're supposed to climb up on that, Jimper," Vallant said. "So they can get a look at us."

"Must we?"

"I guess we'd better—if we don't want to get whisked, like the Haik."

Vallant and Jimper got to their feet, walked across to the ragged-edged, spongy mat, clambered up on it. At close range, the fibres that comprised it were clearly visible; it was like a coarse felt of pale straw.

"OK," Vallant hailed. "Lift away . . ."

They lost their balance as the platform surged up beneath them: a white light appeared, grew. Their direction of motion changed; the paper tilted sickeningly; then, with an abrupt lurch, came to rest. The glare above, like a giant sun, cast blue shadows across the white plain behind them. A mile away, two unmistakable faces loomed, block-long eyes scanning the area, their changing shapes even more alarming at close range.

"*There it is!*" A shape like a vast blimp floated into view, pointing.

"*Yes—and isn't that another one beside it—a hatchling, perhaps?*"

"*Ah, poor things; a mother and young. Always have I had a soft spot for maternity.*"

"Here—" Jimper started.

"Quiet," Vallant hissed. "I'd rather be a live mother than whisked."

"Size is not all," Jimper peeped indignantly.

"*Now, small ones. Perhaps you'll tell us of your*

tiny lives—your minuscule affairs, your petty sorrows and triumphs; and who knows? Maybe there'll be a lesson therein for wise T'tun to ponder."

"How can it be that they know the speech of the Spril?" Jimper chirped.

"They don't—it's some kind of telepathy; it comes through as English, for me."

"Here—natter not among yourselves; explain your presence—"

"Not so harshly, Yapud; you'll frighten the tiny things."

"None so quick to fear are we!" Jimper piped. "Know that we have passed through many strange adventurings, and no enemy yet has seen our heels!"

"Ah, this could prove diverting! Start at the beginning, bold mite; tell us all."

"Very well," Jimper chirped. "But at the end of my recital, hopeful I am you'll hold out aid to two poor travelers, lost far from home."

"These fleas wish to bargain?"

"The offer is fair. Begin."

"When Jason the Giant would leave fair Galliale to seek again his homeland," Jimper chirped, "Jimper was chosen to travel at his side . . ."

There was a moment of silence when Jimper, assisted at points by Vallant, had finished his account.

"So," the being called Yapud said, *"The mind-fleas admit they burrowed a path through our-walls—"*

"A remarkable achievement, for such simple creatures," Brometa said calmly.

"Hmmph! I see nothing remarkable in the series of blundering near-disasters these fleas managed to devise for themselves; why, even a slight exercise of intelligent effort would have aligned their environment correctly—"

"*Yes, Yapud, I've been puzzling over that; and I think I have the answer; these tiny mites dwell in a three-dimensional space—*"

"*Spare me your allegorical apologia—*"

"*I'm being quite objective, Yapud! These entities —intelligent entities, too, mind you—are confined to a three dimensional frame of reference; obvious relationships are thus forever beyond their concep-tualization.*"

Vallant and Jimper stood together, watching the vast faces change and writhe like shapes of smoke as the creatures conversed.

"Remind them of their promise, Vallant," Jimper chirped.

Vallant cleared his throat. "Ah . . . now, about our difficulty; you see—"

"*You mean,*" Yapud said, ignoring him, "*that they crawl about, cemented to a three-dimensional space, like so many Tridographs?*"

"*Precisely! As we move about, presenting various three-dimensional views to their gaze, our appear-ances must seem to alter quite shockingly. Of course, the concept of viewing our actual forms in the hyper-round, from outside, as it were, is quite beyond them!*"

"*Poof! You're quite wrong; you've already ad-mitted they tunneled into the Hall, which certainly required manipulation in at least four dimensions!*"

"*Hmmm.*" Another pause. "*Ah, I see: the tunnel was punched through their space by another more advanced species; look for yourself, Yapud.*"

There was another pause. "*Well . . . yes, I see what you mean. . . . Odd. . . . Did you notice the orientation of the tunnel?*"

"*No, I hadn't—but now that you mention it, I'm beginning to see why these poor creatures have had such a time of it . . .*"

"Please, fellows, if you don't mind," Vallant spoke up. "My friend and I are hoping you'll be able to help us out; you see, it's very important that we get back——"

"That, of course, is out of the question," Yapud interrupted. *"We'll swat these fleas and plug the hole, and then on to other matters . . ."*

"Not so fast, my dear Yapud. The energies required to plug the tunnel would be quite fantastic. You realize, of course, that it constitutes an infinitely-repeating nexus series——"

"All this is very interesting, I'm sure," Vallant put in, "but unfortunately, it's over our heads. Couldn't you just direct us back to our-uh-tunnel——"

"That would do you no good; you'd end in Null space——"

"But it leads to the Tower of the Portal——"

"Surely you understand that since you're traversing a series of tri-valued pseudo-continua, via—— Dear me, I'm afraid you won't be able to grasp the geometry from your unfortunate three-dimensional viewpoint. But——"

"Here, Brometa, you're only confusing things. Place yourself in their frame of reference, as you suggested yourself a moment ago. Now——"

"But the Portal opened from the Tower; it *has* to lead back there——" Vallant insisted.

"Tsk tsk; three-dimensional thinking. No, the tunnel was devised as a means of instantaneous travel between points apparently distant to a tri-dimensional being. Naturally, the energy displaced by such a transposition required release; thus, a non-entropic vector was established to a locus bearing a temporal relationship to the point of origin proportional to the value of C."

"Here," Vallant said desperately. "We're not getting anywhere. Could I just ask a few questions—and could you answer in three-D terms?"

"*Very well. That might be simpler.*"

"Where are we?"

"*Ummm. In the Hall of the T'tun, in the Galaxy of Andromeda—and don't say you don't understand; I plucked the concepts from your own vocabulary.*"

Vallant gulped. "Andromeda?"

"*Correct.*"

"But we were on Galliale—"

"*The use of the past tense is hardly correct, since the Portal you used will not be constructed for three million years—in your terms, that is.*"

"I'm not sure my terms are equal to the job," Vallant said weakly. "How did we happen to get into the past?"

"*The velocity of light is a limiting value; any apparent exceeding of this velocity must, of course, be compensated for. This is accomplished by the displacement of mass through quaternary space into the past to a distance equal to the time required by light to make the transit. Thus, an 'instantaneous' transit of ten light years places the traveler ten years in the subjective past, relative to the point of origin—three-dimensionally speaking.*"

"Ye Gods!" Vallant swallowed. "Andromeda is over a million light years from Earth; when I went through the Portal, I stepped a million years into the past?"

"*A million and a half, to be precise.*"

"But—when the Illimpi came to Galliale through the Portal, they didn't go into the past—or did they?"

"*Oh, I see; there's a further projection of the tunnel, leading ... Brometa, how curious! The tunnel*

*actually originates here on the site of the Hall! Just
a moment, while I scan through. . . ."*

"Vallant," Jimper piped, "what does it all
mean?"

"I'm not sure. It seems the Illimpi started from
here in Andromeda—and threw a link across to our
Galaxy; then they went through, and colonized Galliale—a million and a half years in their past.
When I stepped through the Portal, I dumped us
another million and a half years back—three million years from Cessus—"

"And, of course," Brometa said, *"the Gateway
between Galliale and Olantea will be a similar link,
when it is built; it will span merely twenty light-
years—"*

"Aha!" Vallant exclaimed. "So that's why no one
ever comes back from the Cave of No Return,
Jimper—they step twenty years into the past when
they go out—and another twenty when they come
back!"

"Then I came back to Galliale forty years ere
I departed?" Jimper squeaked. "Small wonder King
Tweeple was leaner, and knew me not . . ."

"But the Niss—the ones that poured through the
Gateway into Galliale, back when the Giants were
killed off—"

"Twenty thousand years ago," Yapud put in.

"Huh? How do you know?" Vallant said, surprised.

"How? Why, I simply examined the data—"

"Remember," Brometa put in, *"your three-
valued space places unnatural limitations on your
ability to perceive reality. Three-dimensional 'time'
is a purely illusory discipline—"*

"Please, no extended theoretical discourse,
Brometa! I'm answering the flea's questions!"

"So twenty thousand years ago, the Niss invaded Galliale from Olantea—and dropped twenty years into their past in the process. They couldn't go back, because they'd step out into Olantea, another twenty years earlier—"

"—*where they promptly expired, as is their custom when surrounded by their enemies,*" Yapud cut in. "*However, on Galliale, they were successful —for a while. When they came, they blazed a path before them with disruptor beams; then they spread plagues which only the Spril survived.*"

"And then the Spril wiped out the Niss, by hiding and picking them off." Vallant put in. "But . . . the Galliales should have warned the Olanteans; the invasion came from Olantea—twenty years in the future—and they were in communication with the Olantea of twenty years in the past—"

"*They had no opportunity; the Niss held the Gateway. On Olantea, the Niss struck with blind ferocity from space; they descended first on the Olantean satellite; there they set up an engine with the power to shatter worlds. To save the mother world, the Olanteans launched a desperate assault. They carried the Dome under which the Engine had been assembled, and then, quickly, before they could be overcome, they triggered the energies buried deep in the rock. Thus died the moon of Olantea.*"

"What about the Niss?"

"*It was a terrible defeat—but not final. The mighty detonation of the Olantean moon destroyed the equilibrium of the system; vast storms swept the planet; when they ceased, it was seen that Olantea had left its ancient orbit, and drifted now outward and ever outward. Snow covered the gardens and the fountains and the towers of Olantea; the seas*

*froze. A winter came which never Spring would fol-
low.*

"*The Niss—those who remained—struck again;
a last, desperate bid to annihilate their enemies.
They attacked Olantea, seized the Gateway to Galliale, and poured in their numbers through it, fleeing
the cold that now locked Olantea in a mantle of
ice. Their fate you know.*"

"But—what happened to Olantea?"

"*It found a new orbit at last, far from its sun.
You call it Pluto.*"

"And the remains of the moon are the asteroids,"
Vallant said, awed. "But—Cessus said that humans
were related to the Illimpi . . ."

"*Some few Illimpi escaped from dying Olantea
to colonize the Earth. There they lived in peace for
two hundred centuries—until the first flashes of
nuclear explosion summoned the remnant of the
Niss from Mars.*"

"And now they're occupying us," Vallant said.
"Snooping around to find a clue to the Portal . . ."

"*Bah! That would merely provide us with a
plague of the evil nits!*" Brometa burst out. "*That,
we cannot allow to come to pass. We must give
aid to these inoffensive fleas, Yapud—*"

"*True,*" Yapud agreed. "*I confess I was quite carried away, viewing the Niss onslaught and the death
of a world as I did, from the three-dimensional
viewpoint. I see now that even these mites have
feelings of a sort—and the destruction of beauty
is a crime, in any continuum!*"

"I suppose the old man—" Vallant stopped suddenly. "He came back—from Galliale! That means
he went there—after I met him—and then came
back through time, twenty years—"

"*Forty years; twenty when he entered Galliale,
and twenty more on his departure.*"

"And he knew! That's why he waited, Jimper! You said he told the King he couldn't leave until the time was right; he posted sentinels by the Gateway to watch the valley of Blue Ice, and settled down to wait. When the Survey Team landed near the Gate, he had his chance!"

"And knowing he would emerge into his past, he brought me with him to prove that he had indeed visited fair Galliale—"

"But who told him about the Gateway? He—"

"Vallant!" Jimper squeaked. "He came to you, spoke of old days of comradeship, and showed you pictures—"

"Then—that means he *was* Jason—the same Jason I knew!" Vallant shook his head. "But that means I've already—I mean, *will* see him again. But how can I get three million years into the future?"

"Yes . . . that is something of a problem," Yapud conceded.

"Uh—I know it's asking a lot," Vallant said, "but if you could just transfer us ahead through time . . ."

"No . . . we can scan it—as you visually scan space when you stare into your night sky—but as for traveling in substance—or transmitting three-dimensional beings—"

"Wait—I have a thought," Brometa put in. *"You spoke of the three-dimensional framework; why not . . ."* The conversation turned to technicalities.

"Vallant," Jimper piped. "Will I ever see again the towers of Galliale?"

"We'll know in a minute; they seem to be discussing ways and means . . ."

". . . the whisk would be simpler," Yapud was saying, impatiently.

"*These Illimpi,*" Brometa said. "*It's just occurred to me that they're remote descendants of ours, Yapud! We can't allow these Niss-fleas to trouble them.*"

"*Impossible!*"

"*But the relationship is quite obvious, once you examine it—*"

"*Nonsense! Next you'll be saying these fleas are our kin!*"

"*Hmmm. As to that, they appear to be ancestral to the Illimpi—*"

"*Nonsense! They're the degenerate descendants of the Illimpi who escaped from freezing Olantea to Earth!*"

"*True—but later, they crossed space via mechanical FTL drive, and colonized Andromeda; later, they recolonized the Milky Way via the Portal—*"

"*Then it's quite clear!*" Yapud exclaimed. "*I told you the Illimpi were no descendants of ours. These mites are our remotest ancestors!*"

"*Ancestors?*"

"*Certainly; they will set up a Portal here, a few years from now, and use it to retransmit themselves to the Milky Way, an additional million and a half years in the past, and from there, they will reestablish a new link to Andromeda, three million years prior to now, and so on, in order to study their past—*"

"Stop!" Vallant called. "You're making my head ache. Compared to this, the business of Jason and I telling each other about the Gateway is nothing! But how can I start the ball rolling if I'm stranded here?"

"*Obviously, we can't allow that to happen,*" Brometa said. "*There's no telling what it might do to the probability stress-patterns. But as to how—*"

"Just a minute, Brometa," Yapud cut in. *"Place yourself in their three-valued universe for a moment; if the transit were made strictly within the parameters of their curious geometry, the aleph and gimel factors would cancel out nicely—"*

"Why—how obvious! It should have occurred to me, Yapud!"

"Have you thought of something?" Vallant asked anxiously.

"Fleas, if we place you back in your native spaciotemporal coordinates, will you pledge yourselves to purge your galaxy of Niss? We'll prepare a simple pesticide for you; an elementary excitor effect should be adequate; direct it on a Niss and the creature will blaze up nicely, without affecting other forms of energy concentration. I think a range of one light year for the hand model should do . . ."

"I'll attend to preparing a suitable three-dimensional capsule," Yapud put in. *"Rather amusing to realize that these fleas can be confined merely by drawing a plane about them . . ."* his voice faded.

"What are you going to do?" Vallant asked nervously. "I hope you're keeping in mind that we don't live long enough for any really extended processes . . ."

"We'll give you a . . . ah . . . ship, I think the term is. It will travel at a velocity just under that of electromagnetic radiation—and will follow a route which will require three million years for the transit to your home galaxy. Naturally, the subjective elapsed time aboard will be negligible. The duration of the voyage will be adjusted with precision so as to place you in the close vicinity of Earth at the same time that you departed. We'll take a moment to encapsulate the vessel in certain stress

patterns, which will render it impervious to unwelcome interference by the Niss or any others—"

With a whoosh! of displaced air which sent Vallant and Jimper skittering across the spongy plane, a gleaming, hundred-foot hull swooped down to settle gently a hundred yards away.

'I've taken the precaution of installing a duplicator for the production of the anti-Niss weapons," Yapud said; *"just set it up in any convenient location and shovel dirt in the hopper at the top—and stand well back from the delivery chute."*

"One other detail," Brometa added. *"Since the Illimpi will be our ancestors, I think we owe it to them to help all we can. If we nudge Olantea from its cold orbit and guide it back to its ancient position, fifth from the Sun, once more it will flower. There seem to be some fifty million Illimpi still there, carefully frozen in special vaults under the ice, awaiting rescue. We can time matters so that they thaw as the Earth-fleas eliminate the last of the Niss.*

"That should be a joyous reunion. I note that the first of the new colonists will begin to cross to Galliale as soon as the Haik follows the fleas here . . ."

"What of Jimper?" the Spril piped. "Long have I fared from the hills of fair Galliale . . ."

"Don't worry, Jimper. I'll drop you off; you'll arrive home another twenty years in your past, but I guess it can't be helped."

Jimper looked startled. "I have but remembered another fanciful tale, told to me long ago, by the father of my grandfather, when he was well gone in strong ale. He told of venturing into the Tower, and traveling far, only to return at last to Galliale . . ."

"The old boy had a tale for every occasion," Vallant said.

"You fail to grasp the implication," Jimper sighed. "For him was I named, Vallant . . ."

Aboard the ship, Vallant slept for a week. When he awoke, Pluto hung silver-black in the viewport. He brought the vessel in over the Blue Ice Mountains, settled it by the cave, watched as Jimper scampered to its opening, turned to wave, and disappeared within.

Nine days later, he swept past startled Niss patrols to slide into Earth's atmosphere; one alien vessel which came too near plunged out of control into the Atlantic.

Vallant landed in wooded country north of Granyauck, left the ship by night, caught a ride into the city. On the campus of the University Complex, he found the vast dormitory in which Jason Able was housed, followed numbers until he reached his room. He knocked. A tall, square-jawed red-head opened the door.

"Oh, hi, Ame," he said. "Been on a trip?"

"I guess you could say that. Pour me a beer, Jase, and I'll tell you all about it . . ."

MIND OUT OF
TIME

Strapped tight in the padded acceleration couch in the command cell of the extrasolar exploratory module, Lieutenant-Colonel Jake Vanderguerre tensed against the tell-tale bubbling sensation high in his chest, the light, tentative pin-prick of an agony that could hurl itself against him like a white-hot anvil. The damned bootleg heart pills must be losing their punch; it had been less than six hours since he'd doped himself up for the mission. . . .

Beside him, Captain Lester Teal cocked a well-arched eyebrow at him. "You all right, Colonel?"

"I'm fine," Vanderguerre heard the ragged quality of his voice; to cover it, he nodded toward the ten-inch screen on which the clean-cut features of Colonel Jack Sudston of Mission Control on Luna glowed in enthusiastic color. "I wish the son-of-a-bitch would cut the chatter. He makes me nervous."

Teal grunted. "Let Soapy deliver his commercial, Jake," he said. "In a minute we'll get the line about the devoted personnel of UNSA; and there might even be time for a fast mention of Stella and Jo, the devoted little women standing by."

". . . *report that the module is now in primary position, and in a G condition*," Sudston was saying

197

heartily. *"Ready for the first manned test of the magnetic torsion powered vehicle."* He smiled out of the screen; his eyes, fixed on an off-screen cue card, did not quite meet Vanderguerre's. *"Now let's have a word from Van and Les, live from the MTE module, in Solar orbit, at four minutes and fifty-three seconds to jump."*

Vanderguerre thumbed the *XMIT* button.

"Roj, Mission Control," he said. "Les and I are rarin' to go. She's a sweet little, uh, module, Jack. Quite a view from out here. We have Earth in sight, can just make out the crescent. As for Luna, you look mighty small from here, Jack. Not much brighter than good old Sirius. MTE module out."

"While we wait, Van and Les's words are flashing toward us at the speed of light," Sudston's voice filled the transmission lag. *"And even at that fantastic velocity—capable of circling the world ten times in each second—it takes a full twenty-eight seconds for—but here's Van's carrier now . . ."*

"Roj, Mission Control," Vanderguerre listened as his own transmission was repeat-beamed to the television audience watching back on Earth.

"Damn the stage machinery," he said. "We could have flipped the switches any time in the last two hours."

"But then Soapy wouldn't have been able to air the big spectacle live on prime time," Teal reminded him sardonically.

"Spectacle," Vanderguerre snorted. "A fractional percentage capability check. We're sitting on a power plant that can tap more energy in a second than the total consumption of the human race through all previous history. And what do we do with it? Another baby step into space."

"Relax," Jake Teal quirked the corner of his mouth upward. "You wouldn't want to risk men's lives with premature experimentation, would you?"

"Ever heard of Columbus?" Vanderguerre growled. "Or the Wright boys, or Lindbergh?"

"Ever heard of a guy named Cocking?" Teal countered. "Back in the 1800s he built a parachute out of wicker. Went up in a balloon and tried it. It didn't work. I remember the line in the old newspaper I saw: *'Mr. Cocking was found in a field at Lea, literally dashed to bits'*."

"I take my hat off to Mr. Cocking," Vanderguerre said. "He tried."

"There hasn't been a fatality directly attributable to the Program in the sixty-nine years since Lunar Station One," Teal said. "You want to be the first to louse up a no-hitter?"

Vanderguerre snorted a laugh. "I was the first man on Callisto, Teal. Did you know that? It's right there in the record—along with the baseball statistics and the mean annual rainfall at Centralia, Kansas. That was eighteen years ago." He put out a hand, ran it over the polished curve of the control mushroom. "So what if she blew up in our faces?" he said as if to himself. "Nobody lives forever."

"*. . . fifty three seconds and counting,*" Sudston's voice chanted into the silence that followed Vanderguerre's remark. "*The monitor board says—Yes, it's coming down now, it's condition G all the way, the mission is go, all systems are clocking down without a hitch, a tribute to the expertise of the devoted personnel of UNSA, at minus forty-eight seconds and counting. . . .*"

Teal twisted his head against the restraint of his harness to eye Vanderguerre.

"Don't mind me, kid," the older man said. "We'll take our little toad-hop, wait ten minutes for the tapes to spin, and duck back home for our pat on the head like good team men."

"Fifteen seconds and counting," Sudston's voice intoned. *"Fourteen seconds. Thirteen . . ."*

The two men's hands moved in a sure, trained sequence: READY lever down and locked. ARM lever down and locked.

". . . Four. Three. Two. One. Jump."

In unison, the men slammed home the big, paired, white-painted switches. There was a swiftly rising hum, a sense of mounting pressure. . . .

2

Teal shook off the dizziness that had swirled him like a top as the torsion drive hurled the tiny vessel outward into Deep Space; he gripped the chair arms, fighting back the nausea and anxiety that always accompanied the climactic moment of a shot.

It's all right, he told himself fiercely. *Nothing can go wrong. In three hours you'll be back aboard UNSA Nine, with half a dozen medics taping your belly growls. Relax. . . .*

He forced himself to lean back in the chair; closed his eyes, savoring the familiarity of it, the security of the enclosing titanium-foam shell.

It was OK now. He knew what to do in any conceivable emergency. Just follow the routine. It was as simple as that. That was the secret he'd learned long ago, when he had first realized that the military life was the one for him; the secret that had given him his reputation for coolness in the face of danger: courage consisted in knowing what to do.

He opened his eyes, scanned instrument faces with swift, trained precision, turned to Vanderguerre. The senior officer looked pale, ill.

"Forty-two million miles out, give or take half a million," Teal said. "Elapsed time, point oh oh, oh seconds."

"Mama mia," Vanderguerre breathed. "We're sitting on a live one, boy!"

The voice issuing from the command was a whispery crackle.

". . . that the module is now in primary position, and in a G condition," Sudston's distance-distorted image was saying. *"Ready for the first manned test of the magnetic torsion powered vehicle . . ."*

"We passed up Soapy's transmission," Teal said.

"By God, Teal, " Vanderguerre said. "I wonder what she'll do. What she'll *really* do!"

Teal felt his heart begin to *thump-ump, thump-ump*. He sensed what was coming as he looked at Vanderguerre. Vanderguerre looked back, eyeing him keenly. Was there a calculating look there; an assessing? Was he wondering about Teal, about his famous reputation for guts?

"What you said before about spotting the record," Vanderguerre's voice was level, casual. "Is that really the way you feel, Les?"

"You're talking about deviating from the programmed mission?" Teal kept his voice steady.

"We'd have to unlock from auto-sequencing and reprogram," Vanderguerre said. "It would be four minutes before Soapy knew anything. They couldn't stop us."

"Roj, Lunar Control," Vanderguerre's voice crackled, relayed from the moon. "Les and I are rarin' to go . . ."

"The controls are interlocked," Vanderguerre added. "We'd have to do it together." His eyes met Teal's, held them for a moment, turned away. "Forget it," he said quickly. "You're young, you've got a career ahead, a family. It was a crazy idea—"

"I'll call your bluff," Teal cut him off harshly. "I'm game."

Say no, a voice inside him prayed. *Say no, and let me off the hook* . . .

Vanderguerre's tongue touched his lips; he nodded. "Good for you, kid. I didn't think you had it in you."

3

"I've locked the guidance system on Andromeda," Vanderguerre said. The pain was still there, lurking—and the jump hadn't helped any. But it would hold off a little while, for this. It *had* to. . . .

"How much power?" Teal asked.

"All of it," Vanderguerre said. "We'll open her up. Let's see what she'll do."

Teal punched keys, coding instructions into the panel.

"*. . . UNSA Station Nine has just confirmed the repositioning of the double-X module in Martian orbit,*" the excited voice of Colonel Sudston was suddenly louder, clearer, as the big lunar transmitter beam swung to center on the new position of the experimental craft. "*Van, let's hear from you!*"

"You'll hear from us," Vanderguerre said, "You'll hear plenty."

"Board set up," Teal said formally. "Ready for jump, sir."

"*Van and Les have their hands full right now, carrying out the planned experiments aboard the MTE vehicle,*" the voice from the screen chattered.

"They're two lonely men at this moment, over forty million miles from home . . ."

"Last chance to change your mind," Vanderguerre said.

"You can back out if you want to," Teal said tightly.

"Jump," Vanderguerre said. Two pairs of hands flipped the switch sequence. A whine rose to a wire-thin hum. There was a sense of pressure that grew and grew. . . .

Blackout dropped over Vanderguerre like a steel door.

4

This time, Teal realized, was worse—much worse. Under him, the seat lifted, lifted, pivoting back and endlessly over. Nausea stirred in him, brought a clammy film to his forehead. His bones seemed to vibrate in resonance to the penetrating keening of the torsion drive.

Then, abruptly, stillness. Teal drew a deep breath, opened his eyes. The command screen was blank, lit only by the darting flicker of random noise. The instruments—

Teal stared, rigid with shock. The MP scale read zero; the navigation fix indicator hunted across the grid aimlessly; the R counter registered negative. It didn't make sense. The jump must have blown every breaker in the module. Teal glanced up at the direct vision dome.

Blackness, unrelieved, immense.

Teal's hands moved in an instinctive gesture to reset the controls for the jump back to the starting point; he caught himself, turned to Vanderguerre.

"Something's fouled up. Our screens are out—" He broke off. Vanderguerre lay slack in the elaborately equipped chair, his mouth half open, his face the color of candle wax.

"Vanderguerre!" Teal slipped his harness, grabbed for the other's wrist. There was no discernible pulse.

Sweat trickled down into the corner of Teal's eye.

"Interlocked controls," he said. "Jake, you've got to wake up. I can't do it alone. You hear me, Jake? Wake up!" He shook the flaccid arm roughly. Vanderguerre's head lolled. Teal crouched to scan the life-system indicators on the unconscious man's shoulder repeater. The heartbeat was weak, irregular, the respiration shallow. He was alive—barely.

Teal half fell back into his chair. He forced himself to breathe deep, again, and again. Slowly, the panic drained away.

OK. They'd pulled a damn fool stunt, and something had gone wrong. A couple of things. But that didn't mean everything wasn't going to come out all right, if he just kept his head, followed the rules.

First, he had to do something about Vanderguerre. He unclipped the highly sophisticated medkit from its niche, forcing himself to move carefully, deliberately, remembering his training. One by one he attached the leads of the diagnostic monitor to Vanderguerre's suit system contacts.

Fourteen minutes later, Vanderguerre stirred and opened his eyes.

"You blacked out," Teal said quickly, then checked himself. "How do you feel?" He forced his tone level.

"I'm . . . all right. What . . . ?"

"We made the jump. Something went wrong. Screens are out; comlink too."

"How . . . far?"

"I don't know, I tell you!" Teal caught the hysterical note in his voice, clamped his teeth hard. "I don't know," he repeated in a calmer tone. "We'll jump back now. All we have to do is backtrack on reverse settings—" he realized he was talking to reassure himself, cut off abruptly.

"Got to determine . . . our position," Vanderguerre panted. "Otherwise—wasted."

"To hell with that," Teal snapped. "You're a sick man," he added. "You need medical attention."

Vanderguerre was struggling to raise his head far enough to see the panel.

"Instruments are acting crazy," Teal said. "We've got to—"

"You've checked out the circuits?"

"Not yet. I was busy with you." Silently Teal cursed the defensiveness of his tone.

"Check 'em."

Teal complied, tight lipped.

"All systems G," he reported.

"All right," Vanderguerre said, his voice weak but calm. "Circuits hot, but the screens show nothing. Must be something masking 'em. Let's take a look. Deploy the direct vision scopes."

Teal's hands shook as he swung his eyepiece into position. He swore silently, adjusted the instrument. A palely-glowing rectangular grid, angled sharply outward, filled the viewfield: one of the module's outflung radiation surfaces. The lens, at least, was clear. But why the total blackness of the sky beyond? He tracked past the grid. A glaringly luminous object swam into view, oblong, misty and nebulous in outline.

"I've got something," he said. "Off the port fan."

He studied the oval smear of light—about thirty inches in width, he estimated, and perhaps a hundred feet distant.

"Take a look to starboard," Vanderguerre said. Teal shifted the scope, picked up a second object, half again as large as the first. Two smaller, irregularly shaped objects hung off to one side. Squinting against the glare, Teal adjusted the scope's filter. The bright halo obscuring the larger object dimmed. Now he could make out detail, a pattern of swirling, clotted light, curving out in two spiral arms from a central nucleus—

The realization of what he was seeing swept over Teal with a mind-numbing shock.

5

Vanderguerre stared at the shape of light, the steel spike in his chest for the moment almost forgotten.

Andromeda—and the Greater and Lesser Magellanic Clouds. And the other, smaller one! The Milky Way, the home Galaxy.

"What the hell!" Teal's harsh voice jarred at him. "Even if we're halfway to Andromeda—a million light years—it should only subtend a second or so of arc! That thing looks like you could reach out and touch it!"

"Switch on the cameras, Les," he whispered. "Let's get a record—"

"Let's get out of here, Vanderguerre!" Teal's voice was ragged. "My God, I never thought—"

"Nobody did," Vanderguerre spoke steadily. "That's why we've got to tape it all, Les—"

"We've got enough! Let's go back! Now!"

Vanderguerre looked at Teal. The younger man was pale, wild-eyed. He was badly shaken. But you couldn't blame him. A million lights in one jump. So much for the light barrier, gone the way of the sound barrier.

"Now," Teal repeated. "Before . . ."

"Yeah," Vanderguerre managed. "Before you find yourself marooned with a corpse. You're right. OK. Set it up."

He lay slackly in the chair. His chest seemed swollen to giant size, laced across with vivid arcs of an agony that pulsed like muffled explosions. Any second now. The anvil was teetering, ready to fall. And the dual controls required two men to jump the module back along her course line. There was no time to waste.

"Board set up," Teal snapped. "Ready for jump."

Vanderguerre raised his hands to the controls; the steel spike drove into his chest.

"Jump," he gasped, and slammed the levers down—

The white-hot anvil struck him with unbearable force.

6

Teal shook his head, blinked the fog from before his eyes; avidly, he scanned the panel.

Nothing had changed. The instruments still gave their dateless readings; the screen was blank.

"Vanderguerre—it didn't work!" Teal felt a sudden constriction like a rope around his throat as he stared at the motionless figure in the other chair.

"Jake!" he shouted. "You can't be dead! Not yet! I'd be stuck here! Jake! Wake up! Wake up!" As from a great distance, he heard his own voice screaming; but he was powerless to stop it. . . .

7

From immense depths, Vanderguerre swam upward, to surface on a choppy sea of pain. He lay for a while, fighting for breath, his mind blanked of everything except the second-to-second struggle for survival. After a long time, the agony eased; with an effort, he turned his head.

Teal's seat was empty.

8

What did it mean? Vanderguerre asked himself for the twentieth time. What had happened? They'd jumped, he'd felt the drive take hold—

And Teal. Where the hell was Teal? He couldn't have left the module; it was a sealed unit. Nothing could leave it, not even wastes, until the techs at UNSA Nine cut her open . . .

But he was gone. And out there, Andromeda still loomed, big as a washtub, and the Milky Way. It was impossible, all of it. Even the jump. Was it all a dream, a dying fancy?

No, Vanderguerre rejected the idea. *Something's happened here. Something I don't understand—not yet. But I've got data—a little data, anyway. And I've got a brain. I've got to look at the situation, make some deductions, decide on a course of action.*

From somewhere, a phrase popped into Vanderguerre's mind:

"Space is a property of matter . . ."

And where there was no matter, there would be . . . spacelessness.

"Sure," Vanderguerre whispered. "If we'd stopped to think, we'd have realized there's no theoretical limit to the MTE. We opened her up all the way—and the curve went off the graph. It threw us right out of the Galaxy, into a region where the matter density is one ion per cubic light. All the way to the end of space: Dead End. No wonder we didn't go any farther—or that we can't jump back. Zero is just a special case of infinity. And that's as far as we'd go, if we traveled on forever . . ."

His eye fell on Teal's empty seat. Yeah—so far so good. But what about Teal? How does the Vanderguerre theory of negative space explain that one?

Abruptly, fire flickered in Vanderguerre's chest. He stiffened, his breath cut off in his throat. So much for theories. This was it. No doubt about it. Three times and out. Strange that it had to end this way, so far away in space and time from everything he'd ever loved.

The vise in Vanderguerre's chest closed; the flames leaped higher, consuming the universe in raging incandescence. . . .

9

Vanderguerre was standing on a graveled path beside a lake. It was dawn, and a chill mist lay over the water. Beyond the hazy line of trees on the far side, a hill rose, dotted with buildings. He recognized the scene at once: Lake Beryl. And the date: May first, 2007. It all came back to him as clearly as if it had been only yesterday, instead of twenty years. The little skiers' hotel, deserted now in summer, the flowers on the table, the picnic lunch, packed by the waiter, in a basket, with the bottle of vin rosé poking out under the white napkin . . .

And Mirla. He knew, before he turned, that she would be standing there, smiling as he had remembered her, down through the years. . . .

10

The music was loud, and Teal raised his glass for a refill, glad of the noise, of the press of people, of the girl who clung close beside him, her breasts firm and demanding against him.

For a moment, a phantom memory of another place seemed to pluck at Teal's mind—an urgent vision of awful loneliness, of a fear that overwhelmed him like a breaking wave— he pushed the thought back.

Wine sloshed from the glass. It didn't matter.

Teal drank deep, let the glass fall from his hand, turned, sought the girl's mouth hungrily.

11

"Van—is anything wrong?" Mirla asked. Her smile had changed to a look of concern.

"No. Nothing," Vanderguerre managed. *Hallucination!* a voice inside his head said. *And yet it's real—as real as ever life was real* . . .

Mirla put her hand on his arm, looking up into his face.

"You stopped so suddenly—and you look . . . worried."

"Mirla . . . something strange has happened." Vanderguerre's eyes went to the bench beside the path. He led her to it, sank down on it. His heart was beating strongly, steadily.

"What is it, Van?"

"A dream? Or . . . is this the dream?"

"Tell me."

Vanderguerre did.

"I was there," he finished. "Just the wink of an eye ago. And now— I'm here."

"It's a strange dream, Van. But after all—it *is* just a dream. And this is real."

"Is it, Mirla? Those years of training, were they a dream? I still know how to dock a Mark IX on nine ounces of reaction mass. I know the math—the smell of the coolant when a line breaks under high G—the names of the men who put the first marker on Pluto, the first party who landed on Ceres, and—"

"Van—it was just a dream! You dreamed those things—"

"What date is this?" he cut in.

"May first—"

"May first, 2007. The date the main dome at Mars Station One blew and killed twelve tech personnel. One of them was Mayfield, the agronomist!" Vanderguerre jumped to his feet. "I haven't seen a paper, Mirla. You know that. We've been walking all night."

"You mean—you think—"

"Let's find a paper. The news should be breaking any time now!"

They went up the path, across the park, crossed an empty street; ten minutes later, from the open door of an all-night dinomat, a TV blared:

"*. . . Just received via Bellerophon relay. Among the dead are Colonel Mark Spencer, Marsbase commandant—*"

"An error," Vanderguerre put in. "He was hurt, but recovered."

"*. . . Dr. Gregor Mayfield, famed for his work in desert ecology . . .*"

"Mayfield!" Mirla gasped. "Van—you knew!"

"Yes." Vanderguerre's voice was suddenly flat. "In the absence of matter, space doesn't exist. Time is a function of space; it's the medium in which events happen. With no space, there can be no movement—and no time. All times become the same. I can be there—or here . . ."

"Van!" Mirla clung to his arm. "I'm frightened! What does it mean?"

"I've got to go back."

"Go . . . back?"

"Don't you see, Mirla? I can't desert my ship, my copilot—abandon the program I gave my life to. I can't let them chalk up the MTE as failure—a flop that killed two men! It would kill the last feeble spark that's keeping the program going!"

"I don't understand, Van. How can you—go back—to a dream?"

"I don't know, Mirla. But I've got to. Got to try." He disengaged his arm, looked down into her face.

"Forgive me, Mirla. A miracle happened here. Maybe . . ." Still looking into her face, he closed his eyes, picturing the command cell aboard the MTE, remembering the pressure of the seat harness across his body, the vertigo of weightlessness, the smell of the cramped quarters, the pain . . .

12

. . . the pain thrust at him like a splintered lance. He opened his eyes, saw the empty chair, the blank screens.

"Teal," he whispered. "Where are you, Teal . . . ?"

13

Teal looked up. An old man was pushing through the crowd toward the table.

"Come with me, Teal," the old man said.

"Go to hell!" Teal snarled. "Get away from me, I don't know you and I don't want to know you!"

"Come with me, Teal—"

Teal leaped to his feet, caught up the wine bottle, smashed it down over the old man's head. He went down; the crowd drew back; a woman screamed. Teal stared down at the body . . .

. . . He was at the wheel of a car, a low-slung, hard sprung powerhouse that leaped ahead under his foot, faster, faster. The road unreeled before him, threading its way along the flank of a mountain. Ahead, tendrils of mist obscured the way. Suddenly, there was a man there, in the road, holding up his hand. Teal caught a glimpse of a stern, lined face, grey hair—

The impact threw the man fifty feet into the air. Teal saw the body plummet down among the treetops on the slope below the road in the same instant that the veering car plunged through the guardrail . . .

. . . the music from the ballroom was faint, here on deck. Teal leaned against the rail, watching the lights of Lisboa sliding away across the mirrored water.

"It's beautiful, Les," the slim, summer-gowned woman beside him said. "I'm glad I came . . ."

An old man came toward Teal, walking silently along the deck.

"Come with me, Teal," he said. "You've got to come back."

"No!" Teal recoiled. "Stay away, damn you! I'll never come back!"

"You've got to, Teal," the grim old man said. "You can't forget."

"Vanderguerre," Teal whispered hoarsely. "I left you there—in the module—sick, maybe dying. Alone."

"We've got to take her back, Teal. You and I are the only ones who know. We can't let it all go, Teal. We owe the program that much."

"To hell with the program," Teal snarled. "But you. I forgot about you, Jake. I swear I forgot."

"Let's go back now, Les."

Teal licked his lips. He looked at the slim girl, standing, her knuckles pressed against her face, staring at him. His eyes went back to Vanderguerre.

"I'm coming of my own free will, Jake," he said. "I ran—but I came back. Tell them that."

14

"Not . . . much time . . ." Vanderguerre whispered as he lay slack in the chair. "Enough . . . for one more . . . try. Out here . . . the MTE can't do it . . . alone. We . . . have to help."

Teal nodded. "I know. I couldn't put it in words, but I know."

"Solar orbit," Vanderguerre whispered. "One microsecond after jump."

"Jake—it just hit me! The jump will kill you!"

"Prepare for jump," Vanderguerre's voice was barely audible. "Jump!"

Their hands went out; levers slammed home. Mighty forces gripped the Universe, twisted it inside out.

15

". . . *that the module is now in primary position, and in a G condition*," the faint voice of Colonel Sudston crackled from the screen.

Teal looked across at Vanderguerre. The body lay at peace, the features smiling faintly.

Teal depressed the xmit button. "MTE to Mission Control," he said. "Jump completed. And I have the tragic honor to report the death of Lieutenant Colonel Jacob Vanderguerre in the line of duty . . . ."

16

. . . He knew, before he turned, that she would be standing there, smiling as he had remembered her, down through the years.

"Van—is anything wrong?" Mirla asked.

"Nothing," Vanderguerre said. "Nothing in this Universe."